RETURN TO FINKLETON

KC HILTON

ReTurn To FinKleTon

KC HiLton

Return to Finkleton
Copyright © 2012 Katrina Chilton
Book Cover Design by Robin Ludwig Design Inc.
Copyright of excerpt material is held by the individual authors.

ISBN-13: 978-1469901084
ISBN-10: 1469901080
Library of Congress Control Number: 2012900653
CreateSpace, North Charleston, SC

This book is a work of fiction. Names, characters, places and incidents are products of the author's imagination or are used fictitiously. Any resemblance to actual events, locales, or persons living or dead, is entirely coincidental.

∾

AWARDS
The Magic of Finkleton

Literary Classics Announces Youth Media Top Book Award Winners
RAPID CITY, SD-

Literary Classics announced its 2011 selection of top books for children and young adults today. Award recipients were selected from entries received throughout the world. The Literary Classics selection committee is proud to recognize the following titles in children's and young adult literature which exemplify the criteria set forth by the Literary Classics Awards committee.

FICTION, PRE-TEEN-
Gold Award Recipient
The Magic of Finkleton
Written by K.C. Hilton

Children's Literary Classics Seal of Approval-

Children's Literary Classics is pleased to announce that the children's chapter book, The Magic of Finkleton, written by KC Hilton, has been selected to receive the Children's Literary Classics Seal of Approval. The Magic of Finkleton takes young readers on an exciting literary adventure. KC Hilton has created a vibrant tale of intrigue which is sure to ignite enthusiasm in the minds of young readers.
-Children's Literary Classics

What people are saying about...

The Magic of Finkleton

The Magic of Finkleton is a captivating novel... K.C. Hilton brings a powerful punch of magic into a fast-paced older children's book that does not disappoint. I found it to be inquisitive, exciting, and truly fun to read. It is rare to find a book so intricately written in which the reader is actually encouraged to participate. I loved the use of descriptive words; the plot was full of twists and turns, and the depth of the characters was amazingly accomplished. K.C. creates the perfect recipe of magic, adventure and imagination that are all easy to comprehend for older children on up to adult readers. I very much look forward to reading her next novel, Return to Finkleton, and sharing these wonderful books with my daughter as she gets older.

I can easily see K.C Hilton's series as either a television series or a film series comparable to Harry Potter, and I do not say that lightly. She is truly a genius in her mad writing skills, and this book portrays to all audiences who love a little magic in their life.

This is by far, the best novel I have read all year, and if I could have given it ten stars, I would have. Look out world, here comes K.C. Hilton!

Rita V for Readers Favorite

The Magic of Finkleton, by KC Hilton, takes young readers on an exciting literary adventure. KC Hilton has created a vibrant tale of intrigue which is sure to ignite enthusiasm in the minds of young readers.

Literary Classics Book Awards & Reviews

The Magic of Finkleton is a delightful story and an entertaining read that begs to have a sequel. The detail behind the magic is both fresh and creative.

The Magic of Finkleton was a simple tale that was attention grabbing from start to finish, and a fun must read for any age group.

Ramona Davis
Best Children's Books

Hilton tells a creative tale of a magical rural village in England. The author introduces magical artifacts such as hourglasses, scrolls and weathered maps with a perspective that is fresh and unique. A solid, simple read that encourages altruism while remaining lighthearted.

Kirkus Book Reviews

∽

READ HOW IT ALL BEGAN

The Finkleton Series
K.C. Hilton

The Magic of Finkleton
Return to Finkleton
Saving Finkleton

CONTENTS

∽

DEDICATION

Chris, you will always be my Fairy Tale.

To our children and grandchildren,
You bring the magic into our lives.

* * *

~

ACKNOWLEDGEMENTS

Jonathan Evans, brought Finkleton to life with his amazing talent and delivered the perfect audio whisper, "It is a magical place"

* * *

PROLOGUE

Under the watchful eyes of the Finkle children, the tiny village of Finkleton continued to flourish with an abundance of crops. And for two years in a row, the weather remained perfect.

Unfortunately, sometimes perfection is wrecked by those with selfish motives. There were people who would stop at nothing to acquire land in Finkleton. However wrong it may be, greed can become an overwhelming hunger. The smallest desire can lead to the most loathsome acts.

Of course, there were also those determined to protect the little village from greedy outsiders.

It was only a matter of time before those who cared about Finkleton and those who cared only for themselves would come into conflict. The result of this outcome would likewise depend on a matter of time.

Those who protected Finkleton were the very same people who could make things right where they once went wrong. The hands of time cannot be controlled. Or can they?

* * *

∽

CHAPTER 1

THE VALLEY OF FINKLETON

You'll never forget a memorable sight.

—Harry Finkle

"Let's go, children! Hurry along now. Darkness is upon us, so we must hurry," William said, urging his family along.

"William, dear," Emma said. "Why on earth have you brought us to the top of the valley? It's nearly nightfall, and the children need to wash up before settling down for the night." Emma stepped over some fallen twigs on the ground.

"I must agree with Mother. Walking in the forest isn't my idea of having fun," Lizzy said, scrunching her face. "What about wolves or some other dreadful creatures? We could be devoured!"

"What's wrong, Lizzy?" Robert asked in a teasing voice. "Are you afraid of the dark?"

Jack laughed at his younger brother. "It's you who's more afraid of the dark, Robert."

William reached the top of the valley before his family. He smiled and then looked back at them. "Not to worry, children. Nothing is going to harm us. Where's your sense of adventure?"

"Oh, William," Emma said. "What sort of adventure brings us into the forest at nightfall?"

"It's a surprise!" William said. "This happens every summer, but with the move and getting settled, it completely slipped my mind. Hurry!" William patiently waited until they reached him. "Now feast your eyes on this!" William stretched his arms out, pointing to the valley below.

"Oh dear!" Emma exclaimed.

"It's amazing!" Lizzy and Robert said at the same time.

"What exactly is it?" Jack asked.

"It's glowworms!" William said with a newfound energy. "Thousands of them will be brightening the land every evening this summer. Other places are lucky to see them every two or three years. No one knows why, but the glowworms are drawn to Finkleton and have made it their home. My father brought me up here when I was a child. We sat here all night and admired the wonder of their light. It's one of my favorite memories."

"It looks like twinkling stars! It's so beautiful," Lizzy said, admiring the view. "I could definitely stay here all night!"

"Yes, I agree," Emma said, then wrapped her arm around Lizzy, pulling her in for a hug. "It is a beautiful sight."

"My father wrote a poem and gave it to me after we came up here. I've kept it all these years," William said, pulling out a folded piece of parchment. He opened it and began to read aloud:

> *Nestled in the valley below*
> *the land is impossibly aglow.*
> *A green, shimmery cast of light*
> *shines out to paint the blackness of night.*
> *'Tis a wonder that makes us forget the tragic*
> *And embrace the goodness of Finkleton's magic.*

"That was beautiful, Father," Lizzy said.

"It truly is a magical place!" Robert whispered.

Jack nudged him in his side, then smiled.

After a long silence, William cleared his throat. "Did I ever tell you about the time it snowed in Finkleton?"

"What's so special about it snowing in Finkleton? It snows all over England during the cold months, Father," Lizzy said.

William laughed out loud, then stopped when he had her full attention. "It doesn't always snow during only the winter months, my dear."

"What do you mean, Father?" Robert asked, now curious.

"It was a long time ago when I was a wee lad, much younger than you, Robert," William said. "We were visiting my Uncle Harry that summer on our yearly holiday. As you know, my father and my Uncle Harry were brothers, and they would stay up late drinking tea and discussing Finkleton. I used to curl up with a blanket and fall asleep under the table." William laughed, remembering.

4

"But here's what you don't know," William continued. "One evening my mother was dreadfully tired. She tucked me in early and went to bed. For some reason I couldn't sleep, so I tiptoed down the hall and waited, holding my blanket until my father saw me. He opened his arms, and I ran and jumped into his lap. I told him I couldn't sleep."

"What about the snow, Father?" Robert asked impatiently.

William laughed again. "I'm getting to that, Robert. My Uncle Harry gave me a mug of warm milk and my father took me back to bed. He tucked me in and told me a bedtime story about fairies. I glanced out the window and I saw snowflakes. It was snowing!"

"Are you sure it was snowing, Father?" Lizzy asked, looking skeptical.

"I'm positive, Lizzy," William said. "I pushed back the blankets as fast as I could. My father held me in his arms and we watched it snow. Of course the snow melted before it touched the ground, but it was a wondrous sight. I've never seen snow appear again in summer, but I'll always clearly remember the night it did."

Jack, Lizzy and Robert listened attentively to their father's story, hanging on every word. William told them the most wonderful stories from his childhood.

"My father always told me Finkleton was a magical place," William said. "But I thought he was just spinning tall tales... until that night."

* * *

꩜

CHAPTER 2

MR. WELLINGTON'S BOOKSHOP

Books are a girl's best friend.

—Harry Finkle

L izzy slowly opened the creaky door to the bookshop and stepped across the threshold. The chime of the bell hanging over the door echoed throughout the shop, welcoming her. She took a deep breath, then smiled. Lizzy loved the smell of books and could read them all day. It had taken her nearly two years to read all the books in Uncle Harry's library, and she enjoyed every single page.

Lizzy stood for just a moment to appreciate the books in the shop. There were rows and rows of them on thick shelves almost reaching the ceiling. Between each row was a round window with a spider web design, providing more than enough light for browsing. Lizzy also admired the new titles displayed on the small round tables located at the end of each row.

Since moving to Finkleton, Lizzy and her brothers Jack and Robert helped their parents run the general store, which they'd inherited from their father's uncle, Harry Finkle. Harry Finkle was technically Jack, Lizzy and Robert's Great Uncle Harry, but they mimicked their father and called him Uncle Harry as well.

Uncle Harry was their grandfather's brother. Sadly, Uncle Harry never married nor had any children. He lived in Finkleton his entire life, then unexpectedly died at the age of 82.

Lizzy and her brothers were given pin money to spend as they wished. Jack and Robert would spend their earnings at the local bakery or sweet shop. But Lizzy saved her coins and knew *exactly* what she wanted to purchase.

Every week Lizzy would visit the local bookshop, owned by Mr. Wallace Wellington, and browse the titles. Mr. Wellington was a short, plump man with a very pleasant personality. Of course he wore spectacles, which seemed to be a requirement for bookshop owners.

Mr. Wellington always had something clever to say, unlike other storekeepers who displayed humdrum personalities. His intelligence impressed Lizzy, and his quirky ways made her laugh.

Mr. Wellington allowed Lizzy to sit at a table in the back room and quietly read the older books from the less desirable shelves. Most people wanted to purchase newly published books and didn't even bother to explore the rear of the shop.

Mr. Wellington also kindly lent Lizzy a few books to take home that she'd return the following week. She was more than eager to visit his shop today because not only was she returning books, she was planning to purchase two books he'd been holding for her.

"Hello, Mr. Wellington," Lizzy said, smiling. She handed him the books she'd finished reading.

"Hello Lizzy," Mr. Wellington replied, grinning. "I take it you enjoyed reading my friends?"

Mr. Wellington referred to the books in his shop as his *friends*. He would say, "Friends, I have hundreds of them! Where would I ever be without them? On occasion they leave me bound for a new home, but new friends arrive weekly, so I am never alone."

"Oh yes, I truly did," Lizzy said, "and today I am buying the two books you've been holding for me." Lizzy's face beamed with joy. She could hardly wait to take her books home and place them next to her favorite childhood doll on the fireplace mantel in her bedroom. She'd named her doll Victoria, because that's what little girls do; they name their favorite dolls and keep them forever.

Mr. Wellington stooped below the counter for a moment, then stood holding the books Lizzy had been saving her pin money to purchase. Using a small dust rag he lightly brushed them off, then placed them on the counter directly in front of her.

"You have good taste in friends, Lizzy," Mr. Wellington said, tapping the books with a smile.

Lizzy eagerly removed the coins from her purse and placed them in Mr. Wellington's palm. She then gathered the books up and hugged them close to her. Although she had already read these books, she could read them over and over again and never get bored. These books would become her new friends, as Mr. Wellington liked to say.

"I moved a few more of my friends into the back room, if you'd care to sit a while and have a read," Mr. Wellington added. "Most folks around here only want to read stories of adventures and such, but I have a feeling you'll enjoy some of these." Mr. Wellington smiled once more at Lizzy and then continued about his business.

Lizzy proceeded quickly to the back of the shop. Her fast walk turned into a skip; she couldn't wait to see the books Mr. Wellington mentioned. A young lady should never run, but Lizzy felt skipping was altogether different.

The back room didn't appeal to most folks. Each time Lizzy removed a book from a shelf there, she had to blow a thin layer of dust off the cover before opening it, and sometimes she sneezed.

Above the bookshelves was a small grimy window adorning the longest wall. It permitted just enough light to see the thick cobwebs that decorated the nooks and corners of the room.

Lizzy had once thought about offering to clean the room, but she didn't want to offend Mr. Wellington. Besides, that would have given her less time for browsing books. She enjoyed a room full of books, clean or dusty. She could travel the world by simply reading.

Mr. Wellington had a habit of placing a new candle in the holder right before Lizzy arrived. *He might not take the time to keep this place clean,* Lizzy thought, *but he's thoughtful enough to make sure I always have enough light to read by.*

Lizzy gazed at the books stacked on the floor. She placed her own books on the small rickety table next to the unlit candle, then knelt down to admire the new additions to the neglected room.

The shop bell chimed. Lizzy could hear Mr. Wellington talking to someone. Lizzy didn't pay much attention to the new customer, though; she was too intrigued with the books that surrounded her.

Typically a person would enter the shop and request a new title, pay for the book, and leave. Lizzy never saw anyone besides her hover in the shop for long. Lizzy thought this was kind of sad. Mr. Wellington's shop held thousands of books. She never got bored there.

If I had enough coins, Lizzy thought, *I would buy them all! Uncle Harry's library is already packed full of books, but I could make space in my bedroom.* Lizzy loved to daydream about all the books she'd read, and she couldn't wait to read more.

Lizzy had never understood why her brothers, Jack and Robert, didn't like to read. She felt that she'd lose her mind if she couldn't read a book. The idea of a world without books was frightful to her. How else would people be able to learn? And wouldn't they miss the feeling of a book in their hands? Lizzy brushed the unpleasant thought out of her mind.

Lizzy noticed a book titled *Glowworms of Finkleton.* She thought, *How perfect!* She opened the book and discovered all the pages had been written by hand. *This must have been a personal journal,* she thought. *Maybe it was owned by someone who studied insects in Finkleton.*

Lizzy opened the journal. This is how it began:

The glowworms in England never remain in the same place, making it hard to conduct a proper scientific study of their habitat.

A major exception to this rule are the glowworms in Finkleton, which remain in the area and thrive. No one knows why. Perhaps it's the lush countryside, or the perfect seasonal weather.

Whatever the reason, the radiant green light of the glowworms brighten the countryside during the summer. This glorious sight is like nothing else on earth. Sadly, it happens only every two or three years, in other parts of England.

* * *

CHAPTER 3

YOUNG MEN DO READ

Books can begin a conversation.

—Harry Finkle

Lizzy heard footsteps approaching. It was unlike Mr. Wellington to interrupt her while she was reading. Lizzy put down the journal and glanced toward the doorway. Just then a young man entered. Lizzy quickly averted her eyes and pretended to read. *What is he doing in here?* Lizzy wondered.

Lizzy had never known anyone to deliberately venture into the back room of the shop. Usually when people took a look at the untidy room they would immediately turn around and return to the front. This young man was not leaving, however. *Who is he, and why is he here?* Lizzy wondered.

Lizzy peeked above the book she was pretending to read and noticed the young man browsing the shelves. He slid his fingers along the leather spine of each book, removing the dust and reading the title. Lingering in one area, he unexpectedly glanced in Lizzy's direction.

Lizzy didn't realize she'd been staring at him. Her cheeks turned a light shade of pink before she returned her eyes to the book in her hands.

The young man cleared his throat. "Hello," he said.

"Um, hello," Lizzy reluctantly replied. How rude. Could he not see that she was reading? Even though she had been pretending, it was still rude of him to interrupt.

"What are you reading?"

"It's a book about glowworms."

"Glowworms? Why would you want to read about them?" he asked.

"Aren't they just so fascinating?" Lizzy asked back. "Last night was the first time I've ever seen them, and they're wonderful.

"It happens every summer," he said in a bored voice, then continued to thumb through the pages of a book.

"It's like the stars in the sky have fallen onto the valley," Lizzy said dreamily. "It's just so beautiful, don't you think?"

The young man laughed and continued to browse the shelves.

"What's so funny?" Lizzy asked.

The young man cleared his throat again, then opened a book he had removed from one of the upper shelves. "It's just that you're a girl. Shouldn't girls be reading books about love or fairies or something of that nature?"

With one hand Lizzy snapped her book shut. "Whatever gave you that idea?" she demanded. Her blushed cheeks turned bright red. She narrowed her eyes at the intruder and prepared for a verbal fight.

"I'm sorry," he said, to her surprise. "I can see that I've offended you. That certainly wasn't my intention. My apologies." The young man lowered his eyes, then turned around to inspect the book shelves once more.

Silence filled the air. Lizzy reopened her book but merely stared at the words on the page. Had she been too harsh with him? She didn't mean to be rude and suddenly felt awful about her outburst. Taking a deep breath, she decided to break the silence and start anew.

"I don't read stories of love or fairy tales of any kind, because they don't contain real knowledge," Lizzy said in a softer but firm tone. She was very proud of the fact that she enjoyed reading only books with factual information in them.

Lizzy wasn't always this way. When she was a young girl, her father told her stories about fairies and they fascinated her. Her wish was to be able to actually see one. Her father said they were real. Why would she believe otherwise?

That all changed when Lizzy was made the object of ridicule by a group of schoolmates. The children teased her when she retold the fairy stories. She was so deeply embarrassed that she never got over it. From that day forward, she read only factual books and had nothing more to do with tales of fairies.

"They don't contain *real* knowledge, you say? You can't possibly be serious," he replied. "You may not want to read stories of love, not everyone does. But to not want to read about fairies is something altogether different. Fairies are real, and any books written about them *do* contain real knowledge."

The young man returned a book to the shelf and chose another, then turned to face Lizzy and waited for her to respond.

"*You* believe in fairies?" Lizzy asked, laughing. *Who in his right mind over the age of five believes in fairies?* Lizzy thought.

"Docsn't everyone?" the young man replied.

Lizzy stopped laughing. "I don't." *Not anymore,* she thought.

"Maybe you should try reading a book about them. You might enjoy it," the young man said.

"This is one of my favorites," he continued, tapping the tome he was holding. "Each time my uncle comes to visit, he buys me a book or two of my choice. He knows I enjoy reading." The young man returned to browsing.

Lizzy got up and began browsing the books on the shelves too. She thought about what he had said. *Would I enjoy reading a different type of book? Made-up stories appealed to me when I was young, but not anymore. Maybe something is wrong with me! What if I don't have an imagination?*

Just then the shop bell rang once again, announcing another patron. Lizzy glanced toward the shop entrance and gasped. There stood none other than Mr. Lewis Lowsley. *What is he doing here?* Lizzy thought. *I've never seen him in the book shop before. What does he want? I need to leave, and be quick about it.*

"It was very nice to meet you," Lizzy's voice squeaked. "I must be going home now." Not waiting for a reply, she hurriedly left the room. Lizzy headed for the shop door, keeping her head down and eyes glued to the wooden floor. Lizzy didn't trust Mr. Lowsley and didn't want to be anywhere near him.

Ever since the Finkle family moved to Finkleton, Mr. Lowsley kept inquiring about land for sale. He nearly purchased Mr. Cornerly's land two years ago, but Jack fixed the broken lever under the shop counter and Robert stopped the rain.

Robert found the lever shortly after they arrived in Finkleton. No one understood how, but it magically controlled the rain.

When the rain stopped, Mr. Cornerly tore up the contract. Mr. Lowsley was furious and tried to persuade him to sign, but it was to no avail. Mr. Lowsley was not very happy with the outcome, to say the least. Mr. Cornerly's farm had thrived over the two years since then.

Pulling the door shut, Lizzy heard Mr. Lowsley ask, "What books do you have today?" *That's odd,* Lizzy thought. *I hadn't viewed Mr. Lowsley as being the book reading type. Then again, I don't really know him. The only thing I know about Mr. Lowsley is that he desperately wants land here.*

Mr. Lowsley wasn't a farmer, so his persistence in trying to buy land in Finkleton was most unusual.

* * *

~

CHAPTER 4

MISS GINIFER SWEETLY

Never trust an adversary.

—Harry Finkle

Robert entered the large room of the general shop his family had inherited from his Uncle Finkle. He noticed Jack balancing on a shaky three-legged stool.

Robert muffled a giggle, then asked, "What are you doing, Jack?"

"I'm restocking the shelves, like I always do at the end of the day," Jack said. Jack placed a few tins on the top shelf and straightened them one by one. He insisted on everything being neat and organized.

"Have you finished your inspection of the hourglasses and decided to finally come help me?" Jack asked. "Hand me another tin, will you please?"

Shortly after moving to Finkleton, the Finkle children discovered an unusual collection of hourglasses. There was an hourglass corresponding to each farm in the village; and every hourglass magically controlled the weather for its farm! This was the reason the amount of rain for each farmer in Finkleton was always perfect.

Robert was in charge of inspecting the hourglasses at the end of each day. Every hourglass was connected to a string that adjusted how quickly or slowly it ran, and so set the hourglass to provide just the right amount of rain for its farm. If a string broke, or if an hourglass' angle abruptly changed, it could mean disaster for that farm.

The hourglasses weren't the only magical items the children discovered. They also found a note from Uncle Harry indicating a clock in the hourglass room that could manipulate time. They all decided to never touch it, though. Controlling the weather was enough to keep their hands full. Controlling time was another story altogether. Some things were better left alone.

"Here you go, Jack," Robert said, and handed his brother a tin.

Just then the shop bell hanging above the entrance door rang. A young lady carrying a small package entered and carefully scanned the store. When she spotted Jack and Robert at the back, she smiled.

Jack stepped down from the stool and wiped his hands on his trousers. "Hello, Miss Ginifer. How are you this evening?"

Miss Ginifer Sweetly was Mr. Sweetly's younger sister. The Sweetly family made the sweetest sweets in town. Miss Ginifer recently began delivering orders to local shops. Jack and Robert looked forward to her weekly visit. Robert licked his lips with anticipation of eating some new sweets.

"I'm quite well, thank you for asking, Jack," Miss Ginifer replied. "I've brought your order," she added, and stepped forward to hand over the package.

Just then the shop bell rang once again. Mr. Appleton's son, Thomas Appleton, stepped inside and walked over to the counter. The Appleton family grew the most delicious apples in Finkleton. Miss Caroline bought them to make her scrumptious pies. Thomas turned towards Jack and Robert, then tapped his fingers impatiently.

"Thank you," Jack said to Miss Ginifer. His cheeks turned a light shade of pink, and a sheen of sweat appeared on his forehead.

"Would you mind very much walking me home, Jack?" Miss Ginifer asked, and smiled.

Jack cleared his throat, then looked at Robert. "Will you keep an eye on the shop while I'm gone? I won't be long."

"Me? You want *me* to watch the shop all by myself? But I'll be alone." Robert's eyes widened.

"You'll be fine, Robert. You're 10 years old now, and I won't be gone long."

"But Jack, she's a *girl,*" Robert said miserably.

Thomas' laughter immediately filled the shop. Jack, Robert and Ginifer turned towards him.

"I'm sorry. I didn't mean to interrupt your conversation," Thomas said, then coughed to stifle his outburst. "But I think I have a solution to your problem, Jack."

Jack narrowed his eyes and crossed his arms over his chest.

"As I was saying," Thomas continued. "*I* could walk Miss Ginifer home. Your little brother wouldn't have to be afraid. And he wouldn't have to tend the shop all alone."

Miss Ginifer looked at Jack and waited for him to respond.

"That sounds like a fine idea," Robert said, and grinned.

Jack looked at Miss Ginifer, then frowned.

"It's settled then," Thomas said. "I'll make sure to get you home safely, Miss Ginifer. Shall we be on our way then?" Thomas held out his arm to encourage Miss Ginifer's decision.

Miss Ginifer's eyes met Jack's, but neither of them said a word. She then turned to Thomas and said, "Yes, thank you. I must be getting home."

Jack and Robert silently watched Thomas and Miss Ginifer leave the shop. Jack's frown deepened. After they were gone, Jack returned to stocking the shelves and didn't say a word.

"What's wrong, Jack?" Robert asked, handing him another tin.

"It's nothing," Jack said, and paused before placing the tin on the shelf. "It's just that she's a nice girl, is all."

Jack excused Robert to get cleaned up before dinner. Jack then continued to stock the shelves with only his thoughts to keep him company.

* * *

∾

CHAPTER 5

MISS CAROLINE VISITS

Laugh at the annoying things.
It's more fun that way.

—Harry Finkle

The next morning Jack, Lizzy and Robert stayed busy in the shop performing their daily chores.

Jack was reorganizing the storage room to stock the new supplies. He rotated the merchandise from back to front, with fresh supplies going in the rear as they arrived.

Lizzy, with the less-than-eager help of Robert, planned to sweep and mop the entire downstairs, including the shop, office, library, storage room, and hourglass room. This would be at least a full day of work. Lizzy couldn't wait to get started, while Robert dragged behind.

Hours later, nearly finished with the shop floor, Lizzy paused while kneeling and wiped her forehead with the back of her hand. Her knees were hurting and her hands were aching. Considering how long it had taken her and Robert to clean the shop floor, she wasn't sure they'd be able to finish cleaning the downstairs entirely. Some of the rooms might have to wait until the next day.

Swoosh! A sound came from the back of the shop. *Swoosh! Swoosh!*

Lizzy leaned over, then peeked around and saw Robert sloshing the contents of the bucket onto the floor. He wasn't cleaning. He was throwing water on the wooden floor and making a huge mess!

"Robert! What are you doing? That's *not* how you clean the floor!" Lizzy narrowed her eyes. All of her hard work was going to waste. It would take quite a while to clean this up. *He's such a child,* Lizzy thought.

"It might not be the way *you* clean the floor, but it does the job for me," Robert said. "Your way is boring. It's more *fun* this way!" Robert grinned, then soaked the floor once again. *Swoosh!* Robert purposely began to hum an annoying tune, just to irritate Lizzy that much more. And it worked.

"Robert! You're insufferable!" Lizzy huffed. She tossed the scrubbing brush into the water bucket beside her. Soapy water splashed, then spilled over the sides of the bucket and onto the floor, creating yet another mess.

Lizzy pressed her lips together tightly, then rolled her eyes. "Will you ever grow up?"

The entrance bell rang, filling the shop with its cheerful sound and welcoming the first patron of the day. Lizzy wiped her wet hands on her apron to dry them off and stood to greet the customer.

Miss Caroline Florentine shuffled through the door. All her friends just called her "Miss Caroline." Her plump round cheeks seemed to shine with her smile, and her floppy hat wobbled with every laugh.

"Hello, my dear! How are you on this lovely day?" Miss Caroline asked.

"I'm very well, thank you," Lizzy replied.

Lizzy always enjoyed these visits. Miss Caroline loved to talk about this, that and everything, and Lizzy loved to listen. Miss Caroline knew most everything about everyone in Finkleton. She wasn't a gossiper, she just chatted with everyone and they enjoyed talking with her. Miss Caroline had a way about her that made a person feel comfortable. With her cheerful conversation and bouncy personality, she was just as famous as her delicious pies.

"That's wonderful, dear," Miss Caroline said. She patted Lizzy on the shoulder and smiled, then tucked a stray white hair back into her hat. "The shop is looking magnificent. Much cleaner than I remember your Uncle Harry ever keeping it."

Lizzy beamed. When they had moved to Finkleton, the shop had been so dusty and disorganized that she didn't think they'd ever get it into proper order. Now the shop gleamed with clean shelves and freshly painted walls. It no longer had the old smell Lizzy remembered. Uncle Harry would be proud.

"How may I help you today?" Lizzy asked.

"I'm here to purchase more supplies for my scrumptious pies," Miss Caroline replied.

Robert licked his lips. Robert loved all sorts of deserts, and he especially enjoyed eating Miss Caroline's wonderful pies.

Jack entered the shop with an armful of sacks and placed them on the counter. "Hello, Miss Caroline," Jack said, wiping his hands on his trousers and greeting her with a warm smile. "It's always a pleasure to see you."

Miss Caroline giggled, "You're such a sweet young man, Jack." Robert rolled his eyes.

"I don't mean to be the bearer of troubling news, but I noticed Mr. Lowsley in town early today," Miss Caroline said. "I've no doubt he's still trying to persuade folks to sell their land in Finkleton."

"Yes, I caught a glimpse of him at the bookshop yesterday afternoon," Lizzy said.

Jack gave Lizzy a look. "It was nothing, really," she continued. "I slipped out before he had a chance to notice me." Lizzy covered her mouth with her hand. "Oh, dear!"

"What's wrong, Lizzy?" Jack asked.

"Well," Lizzy said, hanging her head, "I was in such a hurry to leave the bookshop when Mr. Lowsley arrived that I forgot the books I had purchased from Mr. Wellington."

"I'm sure your books are still there, Lizzy," Jack said.

"I suppose you're right. I'll visit Mr. Wellington again soon." Lizzy looked at Robert, then at the waterlogged floor, and rolled her eyes. "Robert, you can help Miss Caroline carry her packages home."

Robert immediately stopped humming and looked up at Lizzy. "Me? Why me?"

"Because you're not cleaning the floor." Lizzy glared at the area Robert had been attempting to clean. "You're just spreading the dirt around and making a watery mess." Lizzy placed her hands on her hips and narrowed her eyes, daring Robert to disagree.

"Go on then, Robert," Jack said. "I'll clean this up while you're gone. Just in time for you to make another mess when you return," Jack added, muffling a laugh.

"Robert, I do believe I have one more slice of mince pie left," Miss Caroline said, trying to coax

34

him. "But I'll understand if you're too busy help-ing Lizzy clean the floor. It looks like so much fun."

"You made mince pie?" Robert asked, then licked his lips. "I'd be glad to help you, Miss Caro-line." Without hesitation, Robert scooped up her packages and headed for the door.

* * *

≈

CHAPTER 6

CLEANING AND DISCOVERY

Chores can prove to be quite interesting.

—Harry Finkle

Jack helped Lizzy finish cleaning the shop floor, then returned to the storage room.

Lizzy decided to begin cleaning the library floor next. To do so she'd need to move the chairs and roll up the large rug in the center of the room. It was going to be no easy task, and Lizzy was not looking forward to it. She had previously only swept the dirt and washed the floor *around* the rug, but it was past time to remove the rug and clean it as well.

Lizzy grabbed hold of the small table with both hands and scooted it across the room to the far wall. She wiped her hands on her apron and thought, *That wasn't so bad. I don't need anyone to help me. I'm perfectly capable of doing this on my own.*

The wide leather chairs were next. It took all of Lizzy's strength to move them across the floor. She pushed, pulled, and finally tripped, falling to her knees. *You're a bit heavier than I figured on*, Lizzy thought, but she redoubled her efforts until both chairs were moved completely off the rug.

Wiping her forehead, Lizzy glared at the rug. She imagined the strain of rolling it up without any help.

Maybe I should have made a mince pie for Robert, Lizzy thought. *Then he would have been more than glad to help me with this.*

Lizzy knelt at one end of the rug. She lifted its corner to inspect the dust underneath, hoping there wouldn't be much of it and she could abandon her plan. However, the thick layer of dirt she uncovered demanded that the floor be cleaned thoroughly.

Lizzy dropped the corner of the rug. A swoosh of dust flew into the air, making her sneeze. This wasn't her idea of fun.

She began rolling the rug, taking extra care to keep the ends precisely even. Halfway across the room, Lizzy noticed that an area in the middle of the floor was different from the rest of it. The wood floor remained the same, but lines had been cut through it.

Lizzy continued to roll the rug, glancing at the floor as she went. Pushing the rug became harder, as it was becoming heavier with each full turn.

Lizzy sat back to take a break, then looked at the floor once again. She now clearly saw that a square hole about the size of her palm had been cut into it.

Lizzy stood up to get a better look. It was a door carved into the floor! The door didn't have a handle, which is why it stayed unnoticed. If she'd been cleaning the floor properly, she would have found it years ago.

Lizzy knelt next to the door in the floor, then bent down to peek through the hole. It was too dark inside for her to see anything.

Why would Uncle Harry have a hidden door in the floor of the library? Lizzy wondered. Curiosity got the better of her, and she decided to find out.

Lizzy placed four fingers through the hole, then pulled with all her strength. A cold rush of musty air whirled her hair and filled the room. Lizzy stepped around the hole, steadily holding the door upright. She then opened it fully until the latches caught the door and held it at an open angle.

Without hesitation, Lizzy dropped to her knees and peered into the black chamber. After her eyes began adjusting to the darkness, the first thing that caught her attention was a spiral staircase. A few moments later, she saw beyond it—and gasped.

The entire chamber was filled with books! What appeared to be hundreds of books lined all the walls.

Why were all these books under the floor of the library? Lizzy asked herself. *Well, I fully intend to find out.*

Before lifting herself from the floor she glanced down the dark tunnel and noticed something glowing. *It's a dim white light of some sort. Per-*

haps it's a burning candle? But how could it have stayed lit for years?

Lizzy was desperate to explore this hidden room filled with books. She rushed to one of the candleholders in the library and struck a match to bring the candle's wick to life. The burning flame would shine enough light in the space below the library to allow her to see properly.

Lizzy carefully sat on the edge of the open floor and held the candle in her left hand. She placed both her feet on the first step of the spiral staircase, testing its strength. It appeared to be built sturdily enough.

Lizzy slowly stood, keeping her right hand on the edge of the entrance to steady her weight. She bounced a little on the steps and judged them to be strong enough to hold her.

Conflicted with caution and excitement, Lizzy's heart began to race. She knew she should first go tell Jack, but her curiosity got the better of her. A hidden room full of books! How could she resist? Lizzy couldn't possibly wait another minute, and decided to share the news after her inspection was complete.

With the candle held in front of her and taking one step at a time, Lizzy began to descend the stairs.

She spotted so many books that she became overwhelmed. Lizzy could touch any one of them, depending on the step she stood upon. The books were covered in dust but appeared to be in good condition. They were different from the ones in Uncle Harry's library, and didn't seem to be organized in any particular manner. Lizzy noticed titles about herbal medicines, cities, minerals, and more filling the circular wall.

From the corner of her eye, Lizzy thought she saw something shimmer near her head. She quickly turned to look, but nothing was there. *It could have been a glowworm*, she thought, and then brushed the notion away as ridiculous.

Lizzy continued walking down the staircase. Each step brought her closer to the bright light. Eager to discover its source, Lizzy skipped checking the titles of the rest of the books and descended all the way to the bottom of the staircase. Much to her surprise, the ground was solid and dry.

As Lizzy approached the glowing light, she held her free right hand above her eyes to shade them from the brightness. She then noticed that it wasn't a light at all.

It was a book! A book that glowed brighter than twenty candles put together!

Lizzy stepped closer and ran her finger down the unusually warm spine. She then whispered the title aloud: "Lightning."

* * *

CHAPTER 7

JACK DROPS IN

Some secrets are better told.

—Harry Finkle

J ust then a loud thump from above startled Lizzy. She raised the candle above her head to light the staircase to the library.

"Lizzy?" Jack's voice echoed down the tunnel.

"Yes, I'm down here, Jack."

"And where is *here* exactly?"

Before Lizzy could answer, she heard the sound of footsteps descending the stairs. "I tripped over your rug, by the way. It was nice of you to leave it in the middle of the room."

"Sorry about that. But as you can clearly see, I found a hidden door in the floor and I couldn't resist!" Lizzy's voice echoed in the circular tunnel. "Just look at all these books!"

"Keep it down, Lizzy!" Jack hushed her. "We don't want everyone in Finkleton to know. Why didn't you come get me?"

"I planned to do just that—after I inspected it myself," Lizzy said, grinning with enjoyment.

"What is this place?" Jack asked as he came closer to the bottom of the staircase.

"As far as I can tell, it's a hidden room full of books." Lizzy beamed with excitement. "Isn't it wonderful?"

"I can see it's filled with books, but what I don't understand is why they are all down here," Jack said with a suspicious tone in his voice.

"I found something else," Lizzy said, then stepped aside to reveal the glowing book. The brightness shined in Jack's eyes.

Jack turned his head slightly to the side, then raised his hand to deflect some of the light. "What is it?"

"It's a book! And it's glowing!" Lizzy stepped closer to the book and touched it. "The title reads *Lightning*. And the book is *warm*."

"I'm not sure why it's glowing, or warm for that matter, but it makes me nervous," Jack said.

Lizzy lowered her eyes and regarded the glowing book. She was curious, and wanted to read it more than anything.

"Let's get out of here. We can come down here another day, after the shop is closed and we have more time," Jack said.

Lizzy and Jack climbed back up the stairs to the library. Lizzy turned to watch Jack come out of the hole carrying several books.

"What have you there?" Lizzy asked with a new-found energy.

"Books," Jack said dryly. "I thought you'd recognize them, since you love them so much." Jack placed them on the small table, then closed the door to the hidden room.

"Oh, thank you, Jack!" Lizzy unexpectedly wrapped her arms around him and squeezed, causing him to take a step back.

"It's no problem," Jack said. "I'd like to breathe sometime soon, Lizzy."

Lizzy released her hold, and started bouncing up and down.

"I said I was nervous about the glowing book, but the other ones seem harmless enough. Besides, you might enjoy not having to go to the bookshop every week," Jack said.

"We probably shouldn't tell Robert about the hidden room until we find out what it's all about," Lizzy said, walking around the rolled-up rug. "Help me unroll this and put it back into place. I'll clean the floor another day. I have some reading to do!"

"Good idea. I have other things to do as well." Jack straightened the rug at the far end of the room, then moved a chair into its original place.

Jack and Lizzy turned their heads when they heard the chime of the shop bell.

"I'll go," Lizzy said, opening the library door in a hurry. "I'll finish this up later. No need to help, Jack. I can do it."

"Fine. We'll talk about this later. But no going into that hidden room without me," Jack said. "If you need me, I'll be in the office."

* * *

~

CHAPTER 8

ROBERT EXPLORES
THE LIBRARY

Curiosity can cause unwanted trouble.

—Harry Finkle

Robert was outside the library door, a split second from turning the knob and going in, when he heard Jack and Lizzy talking about a hidden room. They hadn't realized that he'd returned from helping Miss Caroline.

Then Robert heard them say they were *not* going to tell him *anything* about it! Robert hung his head. He let go of the knob when he heard the shop bell chime and footsteps coming closer to the library door. He quietly entered the hour-glass room and closed the door. He put his ear to the door and listened until Jack and Lizzy left the library.

His brother and sister keeping an exciting new secret from him hurt Robert's feelings. They weren't supposed to keep secrets from each other anymore.

Robert decided that if Jack and Lizzy didn't want to share their knowledge about the hidden room, he would learn about it himself. They wouldn't need to tell him anything because he would already know it all.

Robert crept inside the library. It looked the way it always did. Robert wondered where the hidden room was. Had he misunderstood what they had said?

Robert noticed a chair and the small table had been moved to the far side of the room. He walked over to the table and noticed various books.

Books are boring, Robert thought as he slid each one of them aside to read the titles. The large book on the bottom of the pile caught his attention, however. It was old, and the leather spine was tattered. The title read *Book of Memories.* He wondered if Lizzy had read it yet. Robert picked it up and placed it near the library door to take with him when he left.

Robert looked around, hoping for some clue to the location of the hidden room, but didn't notice anything. As he walked around, though, he suddenly tripped and stumbled to the floor, landing on his knees and elbows. He turned to see what had made him lose his footing. The rug had an uneven area slightly lifted from the floor. *There must be something under the rug*, Robert thought.

He went to the edge of the rug and lifted the corner, but didn't see anything other than dirt beneath it. He placed the corner of the rug back down on the floor, then crossed his arms and thought for a moment. Robert dropped to his knees and began rolling the rug.

This isn't easy, Robert thought. The rug was nearly the size of the entire room. After rolling the rug towards the middle of the room, Robert nearly gave up—but then he noticed the cut lines in the wooden floor.

That's it! he thought. Robert continued to roll the rug until the door in the floor was entirely revealed. His arms were sore and he was out of breath.

Robert listened for footsteps coming to the library, but he didn't hear anything. He quickly opened the hatch. A burst of cool air blew his hair back, nearly taking his breath away.

Robert opened the door, dropped to his knees, and placed his hands at the edge of the opening. He gazed down the hole in astonishment. All those books!

Then he saw something odd—a curious light shining inside the tunnel. He couldn't make out what it was, but it helped illuminate the spiral staircase.

Robert's eyes widened with excitement. The stairs were exactly what he needed to explore further.

Robert walked down the steps one by one. *Why would Lizzy and Jack care if I know about this place?* he wondered. *It's not as if I like books anyway.*

When Robert reached the bottom of the staircase he stepped closer to the shining light. A book titled *Lightning* was aglow. It was warm to the touch. *How amazing!* he thought.

From the corner of his eye something caught his attention. He turned his head to look, but nothing was there. *Maybe it was a reflection from the light,* he thought.

Still curious about the glowing book, Robert removed it from the shelf with one hand. He heard a *click* sound. Robert peered into the now-empty space where the book had been.

In the back of the hole, Robert saw a lever. It looked identical to the magical lever he found under the counter the day he and his family arrived in Finkleton. They soon learned that lever controlled all the rain in Finkleton.

"Could you be magic too?" Robert whispered. Without hesitation, Robert reached for the lever and pulled it.

In an instant, loud cracks of lightning could be heard from above, and Robert felt the ground shake beneath him. The lightning was relentless. The striking sounds were furious. Robert's hands began to shake. *I need to check the hourglasses,* he thought. *Something must be wrong!*

Frightened, Robert placed the glowing book back in the spot from which he'd removed it, planning to race up the stairs to the hourglasses. Once again he heard a *click* sound.

Then the lightning stopped. Everything was quiet.

Robert looked at the book and touched it with a shaky finger. "Did you cause the lightning?" he whispered. Robert didn't expect to hear an answer, but he listened just the same.

Robert rapidly climbed the steps to the library and closed the secret door. He began to hear people screaming. Hurriedly he unrolled the rug, putting it back into place. He grabbed the book he had set aside beforehand and rushed out of the library.

Robert scurried into the shop. Jack and Lizzy weren't there. The shop was empty. Was he alone?

"Mother? Father?" he called. No response came.

Robert noticed people hurrying past the large shop window. He could hear people screaming, and others yelling. He looked through the enormous window to see what was causing the commotion. Then he saw it.

Miss Caroline's home was engulfed in a blazing fire!

It must have been the lightning! Robert thought. *And the lightning started when I pulled the secret lever behind the glowing book. This is all my fault!*

"Oh, no!" Robert shouted. "What have I done?"

Robert continued to watch the blaze through the window. The Finkleton Fire Brigade arrived to douse the fire. At least, it tried to. He heard muffled cries as people watched them work furiously. The flames on the thatched roof reached for the sky, and black smoke poured out of every window.

Just then Mr. Lowsley and his two business companions, Peter and Paul, stepped in front of the shop. He heard Mr. Lowsley say, "The lightning created the perfect opportunity. I may very well be able to purchase a home in Finkleton after all. Let's go to the pub and celebrate!"

Tears of guilt streamed down Robert's cheeks. *Because of me, Mr. Lowsley will now try to buy Miss Caroline's home,* he thought. He wiped his nose on the back of his sleeve, then bolted through the shop and up the stairs.

When Robert finally reached his bedroom, he collapsed on the bed. *How can I possibly face Miss Caroline after what I've done?* he thought. *She's such a nice lady, and makes the most wonderful pies in all of Finkleton.*

Robert buried his face in his pillow and cried himself to sleep.

* * *

CHAPTER 9

ROBERT IS FOUND

Sleep your troubles away.

—Harry Finkle

"Robert! Robert! Where are you?"

Robert's name being called over and over awakened him from his nightmare. Before he could raise his head from his pillow, his door thrust open and his mother appeared.

"Robert! You're here!" Emma screamed in relief and scooped Robert up in a tight hug. His mother's tears soaked his face. Then she followed with small kisses covering his forehead and cheeks.

"Where have you been? We've been worried sick!" Emma pulled Robert towards her for another motherly hug.

"I've been here in my room," Robert said. He gulped, and then asked, "What's wrong, Mother?" But Robert already knew what was wrong. He could still see in his mind's eye Miss Caroline's home engulfed in flames.

"I'm just so glad you're all right, love," Emma said. She wiped her tears away. "I'm going to check on your father now. You can go back to sleep, Robert. Everything will be fine." Emma hurried past Jack and Lizzy standing in the doorway to his room.

"What's wrong?" Robert asked Jack and Lizzy. *Mother was talking in circles,* he thought. *Why was she going to check on Father?*

"It's just that..." Jack broke the silence. "We've been looking for you."

"We all have," Lizzy interrupted. "We thought you..." Lizzy turned her head away.

"You thought I what?" Robert asked.

"We thought you were in Miss Caroline's house!" Lizzy yelled. "Don't ever do that to us again, Robert! Do you hear me?" Lizzy turned and left. He could hear her footsteps stomping down the hallway and then her bedroom door slam. Robert jumped from the loud sound.

"Robert, the last time we saw you, you'd left the shop to help Miss Caroline with her packages. You were going to eat some of her mince pie." Jack hung his head and shoved his hands in the pockets of his trousers.

"I did," Robert replied. "Then I came home."

"We didn't know you'd returned, Robert." Jack continued to stare at the wooden floor. "We all thought you were still in Miss Caroline's house. Including Father."

"Father? What about Father?" Robert's voice squeaked.

"Father jumped through the flames into Miss Caroline's house looking for you," Jack said. "First he carried out Miss Caroline. She looked like she was sleeping. Father tried to ask her where you were, but she wouldn't wake up."

For a moment the room was completely silent. Only the ticking of the clock in the main living area could be heard.

Jack continued, "Father started back towards the fire wanting to look for you again. Five men tried to stop him, but he put up a fight and they couldn't hold onto him. People were screaming and yelling. The Fire Brigade finally found him and carried him out."

"Father? Is he all right?" Robert choked out the words, tears filling his eyes.

"He's sleeping," Jack said. "The doctor is looking after him. Miss Caroline is resting at the home of Mr. And Mrs. Baker, the bakery owners, and should be fine. But the doctor says Father breathed in too much black smoke. He's been coughing a lot. The doctor gave him something to help him rest."

"It's entirely my fault," Robert said with a whimper in his voice, then buried his face into his pillow. He heard Jack shut the door and walk down the hall.

The rain lever! Robert thought. *Why didn't I use the magical lever under the counter to make it rain and put out the fire that burned down Miss Caroline's home? What good is a magical lever if during an emergency you forget to use it? How could I have let it slip my mind?*

Everything was quiet once again.

* * *

CHAPTER 10

MISS CAROLINE VISITS

Friends and conversation are always welcome.

—Harry Finkle

The next morning Lizzy was working in the shop. The entrance bell rang and Lizzy turned to welcome the new customer. She was delighted about who it was.

"Miss Caroline! How are you?" Lizzy rushed to her side, and guided her to the table and chairs next to the large front window. "I'll get you some tea."

"Thank you, my dear," Miss Caroline said. She attempted to smile, but her usual chipper ways seemed to have gone away. She had lost her home to a blazing fire.

"How is your father getting on today? I want to thank him for saving an old woman's life." Miss Caroline tapped her hand on the table and sighed.

"He's still resting, and Mother hasn't left his side," Lizzy said. "But the doctor said he should be better in no time and for us not to worry." Lizzy poured Miss Caroline a steamy hot cup of tea.

Just then Robert burst into the shop.

"Lizzy! Have you met Fin yet?" Robert asked, clearly out of breath.

"Who?" Lizzy replied.

"You know, Finian Beanly. Fin! Have you met him yet?"

"You're talking in circles, Robert. I don't have the foggiest idea who you're referring to." Lizzy waved her hand in the air to end Robert's rant.

"Oh, how time flies, Robert," Miss Caroline said sweetly. "I haven't seen much of you lately."

"I've been a little busy," Robert said, fidgeting with his hands.

Miss Caroline folded her hands in her lap. "You should consider slowing down a bit. A little more time would do the trick, I should think."

"Yes, Miss Caroline," Robert said, and turned to leave. Before walking into the storage room, he glanced towards Miss Caroline. Curiously, she was staring back at him. She winked, then smiled as he left the shop.

"Miss Caroline?"

"Yes, dear," Miss Caroline said, turning to bring her full attention back to Lizzy.

"You know everyone in Finkleton. Who is Finian Beanly?"

"He's Mr. Simon Beanly's only son. His mother died during childbirth, and Mr. Beanly has raised him by himself. I don't see much of him, but he seems to be a good-hearted young man." Miss Caroline smiled and sipped her tea.

* * *

∽

CHAPTER 11

MR. LOWSLEY VISITS

You can show a foe to the door.

—Harry Finkle

The entrance bell rang once again. It was Mr. Lowsley, who allowed the shop door to shut loudly behind him. He scanned the shop with his beady eyes and smiled when he saw Miss Caroline.

"How are you on this lovely day, Miss Caroline? I'm sorry to hear about your terrible misfortune. May I be of any assistance?" Mr. Lowsley tipped his hat and grinned.

"It's *Miss Florentine* to you Mr. Lowsley. How could you possibly be of any assistance to me?" Miss Caroline grimly inquired, then calmly took a sip of her tea.

"When you're feeling up to it, I'd like to discuss the possibility of purchasing your house. Or should I say, what's left of your house," Mr. Lowsley said with a sneer, though he hid it with a crooked smile.

Miss Caroline gasped. She placed her teacup on the table. "Why on earth would *you* be interested in my home? It's nothing but a pile of rubble!"

Mr. Lowsley cleared his throat, "As far back as I can remember, my father had always wanted to live in Finkleton. He loved this village, and it was his dying wish that one day I buy land and live here. For many years, I've tried to fulfill his dream."

Mr. Lowsley seems to be sincere, Lizzy thought. *Is it possible we've all been wrong about him?*

"I've just lost my home, Mr. Lowsley. I will think about your offer, but I will not be pressured to sell it to you, or to anyone else for that matter. Do I make myself clear?" Miss Caroline pursed her lips together and glared at Mr. Lowsley.

"Yes, I understand completely, Miss Florentine. You need time after such an event," Mr. Lowsley said. He tipped his hat again. "I'll be around for a few more days, if you happen to make a decision before I leave."

Rain suddenly began to pour down.

"Look at that!" Miss Caroline said. "Where was all that rain when my home caught fire?"

Just then Robert rushed into the shop yelling, "Jack! Jack! I need your help! The hourglasses! It's raining all over Finkleton!"

Robert was taken aback when he noticed Mr. Lowsley and Miss Caroline. Robert's gulp could be heard across the room.

Mr. Lowsley immediately stopped and turned towards Robert. "What was that you said, boy?" Mr. Lowsley demanded.

Robert's lips started to tremble. He opened his mouth and tried to speak, but nothing came out. Before he could respond, Miss Caroline began coughing loudly.

"Mr. Lowsley, might you be a dear and accompany an old woman home? Well, to the Baker's home, to be precise. I'm not feeling quite myself and need to rest for a while. We can have a nice chat about the possibility of you purchasing what's left of my house." She stood, awaiting his response.

Mr. Lowsley glared at Robert, then turned to Miss Caroline. "Yes, yes, of course, Miss Florentine. I'd be more than glad to walk you anyplace you'd like." Mr. Lowsley held out his arm to assist her, then glanced at Robert one last time before leaving the shop.

After Miss Caroline and Mr. Lowsley left, Lizzy spun to face Robert.

"What were you thinking?" Lizzy yelled.

Robert hung his head, "I didn't know anyone was here."

"You may not have known Mr. Lowsley was here, but you knew about Miss Caroline!" Lizzy placed her hands on her hips and tapped her foot on the wooden floor, waiting for an answer.

Robert lifted his head, "How could I possibly have known either of them were here?"

"You spoke to her not five minutes earlier! You barged into the shop asking me if I knew Finian Beanly."

"*Who?* I don't know a Finian Beanly. Why would I ask you about him?" Robert crossed his arms over his chest.

"Robert, you're driving me *insane!*"

Jack stood at the top of the stairs watching Lizzy's outburst. He rolled his eyes. "Not again," Jack mumbled, and walked down the steps.

Lizzy quickly explained to Jack what had happened with Miss Caroline, Mr. Lowsley and Robert.

"I'm sorry, Jack," Robert said. "I honestly didn't know they were here."

"Robert, you're losing your marbles! You spoke to Miss Caroline before Mr. Lowsley arrived," Lizzy said. She narrowed her eyes and glared at him.

"Calm down," Jack said. "I'll try to find Mr. Lowsley and learn if he suspects anything. Meanwhile, Lizzy, please help Robert with the hourglasses. I'll return soon."

* * *

CHAPTER 12

MR. LOWSLEY

Keep a close eye on the backbiters.

—Harry Finkle

"You seem to be getting friendly with some of the local folks around here," Peter said as Mr. Lowsley approached him and Paul in front of the Hogs Nest Pub.

"Friendly, you say? Ha!" Mr. Lowsley replied. "It's purely business, I assure you. If I have to purchase every home in Finkleton, I will!"

"Why would you want to do that? You can't live in all of them," Paul pointed out...and then wished

73

he hadn't. He averted his eyes and kicked a loose pebble on the cobblestone path.

"I know I can't live in *all* of them!" Mr. Lowsley said, irritated. "My father told me there were secrets in Finkleton, mysteries he couldn't explain. He made me promise to purchase land here to get to the bottom of them. I used to think he was a bit crazy. But now I believe there's something very odd going on in that shop. And I'm not going to stop until I find out exactly what it is!"

Paul raised his hand to calm Mr. Lowsley down. "We don't want everyone to know what you're up to," Paul whispered.

"We could sneak inside, when they've gone to sleep," Peter said. "Me and Paul have become experts at these doings. We can find out what you want to know."

"I don't expect that'll be necessary," Mr. Lowsley said. "*Miss Caroline* will come around to my way of thinking. Her home, what's left of it, is close enough to the shop for me to keep an eye on things. I can easily rebuild the house and keep a low profile."

"Sounds like a good idea. But if you ever change your mind, the offer is on the table," Peter said.

"Thank you, men," Mr. Lowsley replied. "Now let's go inside and have a meal."

"Look! The rain stopped!" Paul said.

"What's your point?" Mr. Lowsley asked.

"Don't you think the weather is strange in Finkleton?"

"What are you going on about, Paul?"

"The rain, I mean, sir. It starts and stops like I've never seen. It's just unusual, to say the least," Paul said. Shaking his head, he walked into the pub.

Mr. Lowsley remained outside of the Hogs Nest Pub, pondering what the young boy had shouted in the shop: "Jack! Jack! I need your help! The hourglasses! It's raining all over Finkleton!"

"Hourglasses and rain. A curious combination, indeed. If it's the last thing I do, I will get to the bottom of this." With a determined look, Mr. Lowsley followed Paul into the pub.

* * *

∽

CHAPTER 13

JACK FINDS MR. LOWSLEY

You will be gobsmacked many times.

—Harry Finkle

Jack began walking around Finkleton in search of Mr. Lowsley. He noticed the cold rain had slowed, and then stopped. *Lizzy and Robert must have fixed the problem with the hourglasses,* he thought.

Jack passed Mr. Sweetly's shop and the Baker's bakery. Everything smelled wonderful.

But further down the cobblestone path his nose picked up a burnt smell.

The smoky odor led him to Miss Caroline's home...which was in ruins. It would need to be entirely rebuilt.

Jack kept walking. He soon found Mr. Lowsley standing outside the Hogs Nest Pub with his two companions, Peter and Paul. Jack ducked behind some feed sacks to eavesdrop on their conversation.

"My father told me there were secrets in Finkleton, mysteries he couldn't explain," Jack heard Mr. Lowsley say. "He made me promise to purchase land here to get to the bottom of them. I used to think he was a bit crazy. But now I believe there's something very odd going on in that shop. And I'm not going to stop until I find out exactly what it is!"

Oh no, Jack thought. *I can't let them find out about the lever and the hourglasses. Greedy people in control of the weather could be very dangerous. I must find out what they're planning.*

Just then the men started talking in lower tones, however, and Jack could no longer hear what they were saying.

Jack decided to not tell Lizzy and Robert what Mr. Lowsley had said. *It would only frighten them and make them worry*, he thought. *I'll figure something out on my own. Right now I need to get back to them.*

Jack slipped out from behind the feed sacks and began to walk home. When he passed Miss Caroline's property again, he heard a young lady giggle. He looked around and saw Miss Ginifer.

Unfortunately, she wasn't alone. She was walking with Thomas Appleton. They were talking and laughing together, enjoying each other's company without a worry in the world.

Jack shoved his hands into the pockets of his trousers, lowered his head and continued to walk as if he didn't see them. *It's better this way*, he thought. *No need to interrupt them just to say hello. That would be stupid.*

Finally Jack arrived back at his family's shop. Lizzy and Robert were anxiously waiting for him to return.

"What happened?" Lizzy asked.

"Did you find Mr. Lowsley?" Robert asked.

"The rain stopped. I assume you repaired the hourglasses?" Jack cocked an eyebrow, purposely ignoring their questions.

"Jack!" Lizzy yelled. "Tell us about Mr. Lowsley!"

"I didn't find him," Jack lied. *I don't want them to worry,* he thought. *But I'll need to keep an extra careful eye on Mr. Lowsley and watch his every move.*

"Robert, that was a silly thing you did! Mr. Lowsley could very easily start snooping around and it'll be entirely your fault!" Lizzy huffed.

"Don't be so hard on him, Lizzy. It was a simple mistake," Jack said in a hushed tone.

"His *simple* mistake could ruin everything!" Lizzy exclaimed. "What's going to happen if Mr. Lowsley discovers the power of the hourglasses? What then?"

Jack didn't say anything. What could he say? He had to keep Mr. Lowsley from finding out about the hourglasses. That was his only plan.

"If I could take it back, I would! If I could make Father better, I would! But I can't!" Robert screamed, and headed for the door.

"Where are you going?" Lizzy asked.

Robert didn't answer. He just ran out, slamming the shop door behind him.

"Now you've done it, Lizzy," Jack said.

* * *

∽

CHAPTER 14

CLEARING THE MIND

Strike dumb if the need ever arises.

—Harry Finkle

R obert heard Lizzy ask where he was going, but he purposely ignored her. He felt as if she'd done nothing but scold him, and he was tired of it. He needed to get away from the shop and clear his mind. His deepest wish was that Jack and Lizzy would think of something to make everything right while he was gone.

Robert took a deep breath. The scent of fresh baked bread filled the air. He could hear his stomach rumbling. Robert allowed his nose to lead the way on his mind-clearing walk. Food always made him feel better somehow. Maybe it was just because he enjoyed eating.

The bakery was just beyond Hogs Nest Pub. Its shelves were packed with delicious choices. Robert had no trouble finding wonderful breads and pastries to fill his belly.

After eating to his heart's content, Robert left the bakery. He felt entirely better. None of the bad things that had happened had gone away. But with his stomach full, he could think better.

Robert enjoyed walking on the cobblestone path. He made a game out of it on most days, stepping on every other stone, or taking large steps on every fourth stone. Sometimes he even counted them, but he'd always get distracted and lose track before he was done.

Maybe one day, he thought, *I'll count just how many stones it is from our store to the bakery. Now that's an idea! I could map out Finkleton based on how many stones it was to each shop. It might take a whole day, but it would be fun. I doubt anyone has a clue how many cobblestones are laid out in Finkleton. I would be the first to know!*

Just then someone grabbed Robert roughly by his shoulders. "Come here, boy! I want to talk to you!" It was a man's voice, and it sounded familiar.

Robert wiggled and squealed, trying to get out of the man's clutches. "Let me go! Let me go!" He looked up to see who had snatched him aside. Robert immediately stopped moving.

Standing directly in front of him and looking down with his beady little eyes was none other than Mr. Lowsley. Robert always believed Mr. Lowsley was a bad man, and now he had his proof!

"What's the meaning of this? What do you want with me? Let me go! Let me go!" Robert tried to wiggle away once again, but Mr. Lowsley's hands only gripped him that much harder.

"Stop, I say! Stop!" Mr. Lowsley commanded. "Just listen to me for a moment, boy." Mr. Lowsley loosened his strong grip. "I just want to talk to you. I merely have a few questions that you might be able to answer." Mr. Lowsley grabbed Robert's hand and roughly placed four coins into the palm. "I'll pay you for your time."

Robert's hands were noticeably shaking. He shoved the coins inside his pocket. "What sort of questions?" Robert asked, his voice trembling. "What do you want with me?"

"I'm the one asking the questions, boy," Mr. Lowsley said, sneering.

Robert didn't say a word. He didn't like Mr. Lowsley, and he especially didn't like to be alone with him. He had never been afraid of him, but then again Jack or Lizzy had always been around when Mr. Lowsley came to the store.

"Now that we have that straight," Mr. Lowsley said, and grinned. "Tell me exactly what you meant earlier when you said something about hourglasses and it raining all over Finkleton."

Lizzy was right, Robert thought. *Mr. Lowsley really did notice what I'd said.* Robert hung his head. Then Mr. Lowsley grabbed Robert's shoulders and shook him out of his thoughts.

"I asked you a question. Come out with it, boy!" Mr. Lowsley's temper increased with Robert's silence.

Robert finally found his voice, "It was nothing! I stumble on my words sometimes, is all. I'm only 10 years old. I'm just a kid. Leave me be!"

"Do you know what I think, boy? I think you're hiding something. I think your entire family is hiding something, and that something is in that shop of yours. That's what I think!" Mr. Lowsley's face turned red with fury.

"I...I don't know what you're talking about," Robert lied. Robert hoped Mr. Lowsley would believe him, but doubted he would.

"You're not being honest with me. Now tell me the truth!"

"I'm telling you the truth. I don't know what you're talking about!" Robert lied again. He knew exactly what Mr. Lowsley was talking about. But he also knew that if he told Mr. Lowsley, Finkleton would end up in ruin.

"Do you know what happens to people who lie to me, boy?" Mr. Lowsley asked threateningly.

Robert remained silent. He didn't want to know the answer.

"Well, their families do. And you wouldn't want anything to happen to your family, now would you, boy?" Mr. Lowsley's grip tightened on Robert's shoulders.

"No. No, I wouldn't." Robert's voice squeaked, and he fought back tears.

"I'll give you a few days to think about our private conversation. I'm also giving you fair warning to not breathe a word of this to *anyone*. Do you hear me, boy?"

Mr. Lowsley released Robert's shoulders and shoved him back. Then he grinned. "I'll see you in a few days." Mr. Lowsley's beady little eyes glared at Robert for just a moment more before he turned and walked away.

Robert remained still as he watched Mr. Lowsley stroll down the cobblestone path. As soon as Mr. Lowsley was out of sight, Robert trembled uncontrollably. He wiped his sweaty palms on his shirt and took a deep breath to calm down. He could barely take in what had just happened.

I have to get back to the shop to tell Jack and Lizzy. They'll know what to do! Robert thought.

Then Robert had another thought. *No, wait! Mr. Lowsley warned me to not tell anyone. I don't want anything to happen to my family!*

What am I going to do? he wondered. Robert couldn't make his feet move forward; he felt like there was danger in every direction. So he just stood there and trembled even more.

* * *

CHAPTER 15

ROBERT'S REGRET

Books are curious things. They're rarely wrong.

—Harry Finkle

R obert finally managed to make his feet work and get him back to the shop.

Robert didn't say a word to Jack and Lizzy about Mr. Lowsley. Instead, he entered the hourglass room and slammed the door. He fought back tears, wiping his eyes furiously to keep the impulse to cry at bay.

Robert wished Lizzy and Jack would stop scolding him. He wished they'd understand that he had just made a mistake. He didn't mean to talk about the hourglasses in front of Miss Caroline...and especially Mr. Lowsley.

And now Mr. Lowsley was asking him questions and threatening his whole family.

I'm sorry for what I've done, Robert thought. *If I could take it all back, I would!*

But he couldn't take any of it back. Robert's stomach was in knots. Without Jack and Lizzy's help, he felt all alone.

Robert sat at the desk of the hourglass room, placed his crossed arms on it in front of him, and buried his head on his arms. Then his right hand felt something. It was the book that he'd found in the library. With everything that had happened, Robert had forgotten all about it.

Robert didn't care much for reading. When he tried to spend time with a book, it made him sleepy because he quickly got bored. Lizzy was the book lover of the family.

This book was strangely interesting to Robert, though. It was very old and worn. The course leather felt brittle in his hands. And he liked the title: *Book of Memories.*

Suddenly curious, Robert sat up straight and opened the book. The pages were blank!

Is this for a diary or something? Robert wondered. He slid his hand down one of the blank pages. "You're an odd thing. What are you all about?" Robert asked in a whisper.

All of a sudden, letters began to appear in a swirling motion on the page. It was as if someone was stirring a bowl of soup made with letters from the alphabet. Robert couldn't believe his eyes. He blinked several times to make sure he wasn't seeing things.

One by one, the letters spelled out words, until a full sentence presented itself.

Robert read the sentence aloud: "I am a collector of memories."

Robert reared back with a start. "Whoa!" He touched the page to make sure it was real. "How is this possible?" he asked out loud.

"What would you like to know?" read the next sentence from the swirling letters on the page.

Robert stared in awe. *A magical book!* He thought. *A real magical book!*

Robert held his tongue. He wasn't sure what to say next. He tried to remain calm and reason it through.

Robert leaned closer to the book and asked the first question that came to his mind: "Did Jack find Mr. Lowsley?"

Robert believed his brother. In his experience, Jack always told him the truth. But Robert figured this was a good way to test the book, because the right answer had to be "no."

The letters swirled and then spelled out one word: "Yes."

"What?" exclaimed Robert. "Jack said he didn't find Mr. Lowsley. You must be lying!"

The book didn't respond.

"Huh," said Robert. "Either you're mad at me and have stopped speaking to me...or you only reply when someone asks you a question."

The book didn't respond.

"Okay," said Robert. He felt a bit silly talking to a book; but something magical was happening and he needed to find out more. "Are you sure Jack found Mr. Lowsley?"

Sketchy lines began to appear on the empty page. The book was drawing a picture! It showed

Jack hiding behind a bunch of feed sacks and Mr. Lowsley nearby talking to Peter and Paul.

On the opposite page letters began swirling again. After a while they gathered into sentences... that formed, word for word, Mr. Lowsley's conversation with his companions!

Robert was shocked. "Jack really did lie to me and Lizzy! He's never lied to us before. I don't understand why he'd keep something this important from us!"

Robert thought more about it. "Jack and Lizzy didn't tell me about the hidden room full of books. Jack lied to me and Lizzy about finding Mr. Lowsley. And I'm not telling Jack and Lizzy about the lightning lever and the threat from Mr. Lowsley. We're all keeping secrets from each other."

Robert continued talking things out to the patiently listening book. "If I hadn't decided to sneak into the library, I wouldn't have found the glowing book. I wouldn't have been tempted to pull the lever that creates lightning."

"Because I pulled the lever, lightning burned down Miss Caroline's home. Even worse, Father is sick in bed from breathing the bad smoke. And to top everything off, I've all but told Mr. Lowsley about the magical hourglasses, when the most important job I have is keeping them a secret."

Robert reached out to the book again. "Thank you for listening to me. You've been helpful." He closed the magical book—and finally allowed the tears to fall down his cheeks.

The tears kept flowing until Robert was all cried out. He then wiped his cheeks with the sleeve of his shirt. Robert placed the *Book of Memories* in the bottom drawer of the desk drawers for safekeeping.

"If only I could get past all this," Robert said. "Over time Father will be better, Miss Caroline will have her home again, and Mr. Lowsley will forget about me. Things can only get better as time goes on."

At that moment, something in Robert's mind clicked. "Wait a second. Maybe I *can* get past this. I can use the magical clock!"

Robert stood and looked at the clock on the wall in the hourglass room. "Do you truly control time?" he asked. The clock just kept ticking.

"Well, I guess it's time to find out," Robert whispered.

* * *

CHAPTER 16

TEST OF TIME

Today is tomorrow's yesterday. Don't believe it.

—Harry Finkle

Robert stood on the chair to be eye level with the clock. He touched the clock with one finger, then pulled it away. *Will this work?* He wondered. *Can I get past all of these bad things?*

Robert got a determined look on his face. "It *has* to work," he whispered. "It just has to! There's no other way."

Robert reached for the clock again. He lightly placed a finger on the large minute hand and turned it forward slowly. Then he let go.

Robert didn't feel any different. He looked around the hourglass room. *Everything seems the same,* he thought.

Robert put his finger on the large minute hand once more, and turned it and turned it and turned it. Finally, he let go.

"Everything still looks the same," he said, with great frustration in his voice.

Robert stepped down from the chair, left the hourglass room and walked into the shop. It was empty. He glanced out the large window and noticed that the sun had gone down. He wondered how long he'd been crying.

Robert returned to the hourglass room and stood back on the chair. This time he reached for the clock's smaller hour hand. He turned it slowly, then a little faster, and then faster and faster. Robert kept turning the hand, but he still didn't feel any different.

"It has to work!" Robert whispered. He continued to turn the clock hand forward, round and round and round. Nothing noticeable happened.

Robert felt a dull pang of disappointment in the pit of his stomach. "I guess you don't control time after all," he said to the clock.

Carelessly, Robert continued to turn the hour hand over and over and over while he tried to figure things out. "I'll have to tell Jack and Lizzy they were all wrong about you. But wait, then they'll be mad at me for meddling with you. I'm not even supposed to touch you. No, I won't tell them. This will just be another secret."

Suddenly Robert heard a noise inside the clock. It wasn't a good noise; it sounded like a spring breaking. "Well, you're an old clock," Robert said. "I'm surprised you even manage to show the right time of day." Robert finally let go of the hour hand.

All at once, both of the clock's hands flew across the room. They were followed by several small springs and other mechanisms from inside the clock.

Robert didn't feel so well. He touched his head; the room was spinning. He stumbled off the chair and balanced himself, holding onto the desk until the room stopped moving. He rubbed his eyes and looked at the clock again.

That's strange, Robert thought. *I'm not standing on the chair anymore, but I'm still at eye level with the clock.*

Cautiously, Robert turned to face the hourglasses. The shelves looked as if they'd been lowered. Something definitely wasn't right.

Robert looked around the room. It appeared to be smaller than before. *How could the room have shrunk?* Robert wondered.

He noticed the tiny pieces of the clock scattered about the floor. *I've broken it!* He thought. *I'll have to ask Jack to help me fix it. Great, another reason for Lizzy and Jack to be mad at me.*

Robert turned and left the room. *So much for that,* he thought. *The clock didn't do its job, and now it's broken. What more could go wrong?*

Robert walked into the shop. Since it was empty a few minutes ago, and it was still dark outside, he expected to be alone, but he heard a noise. *How strange,* he thought. *Did I imagine that?*

Then Robert heard it again. He peeked around one of the displays and saw a man about his father's age moving things on the shelves.

"Can I help you?" Robert asked. He immediately noticed something else wrong. His voice sounded low. *I must be coming down with a cold.* He cleared his throat.

The man spun around, then smiled, "There you are, Robert. I didn't hear you come in. I've been waiting for you. Can you help me with these?"

Robert took a few steps back. The man *looked* familiar and *sounded* familiar...but who was he?

Robert placed a hand on the wall to prop himself up and rubbed his forehead. He wasn't feeling well at all.

Robert glanced at his hand. It was larger than it was supposed to be. Robert inspected it, front and back. *What's happened to my hand?* He wondered with alarm.

He noticed the small mirror hanging from the wall. It was also lower than it was supposed to be.

Robert looked in the mirror...and gasped. *That's not me!* He thought. *It's someone else entirely!*

Robert brought both hands to the sides of his face. He turned his head slightly to the left, then to the right.

Is this really me? Robert thought. *If it is, then the clock must have worked. I'm in the future! But...I'm old! I'm only 10 years old, but the man staring back at me is ancient! This isn't what I wanted at all!*

"What's wrong, Robert?" the familiar man asked.

"Nothing. Nothing is wrong. I'm just not feeling well." Robert cleared his throat again. *This will take some getting used to,* he thought.

"Well, go on upstairs and rest for a while. I'll finish up down here," the man said, smiling.

"Jack?" Robert asked, looking the man in his eyes.

"Yes," Jack replied.

"What happened to you?"

"What happened to me? What on earth do you mean?" Jack replied.

"You're so...so *old.*"

Jack laughed. "I'm only 41 years old. I couldn't stay young forever. Besides, you've grown old with me, Robert." He continued to laugh. "Go on upstairs and rest a while. You must be overtired."

Robert's eyes widened, and his mouth dropped opened. *If Jack is now 41 years old, that means I'm 35 years old! I turned the hands of the clock 25 years into the future!*

"Where's Lizzy?" Robert asked. It was the only thing he could think to say.

"You really must be tired, Robert," Jack said, laughing again. "Lizzy is at home with her husband and children, of course."

Husband and children? Lizzy is married and has children? Robert rubbed his temples hard.

"Who did she marry?" Robert asked. He was really curious.

"Fin," Jack replied, concern crossing his face. "Finian Beanly. Are you sure you're all right, Robert? Do you want me to fetch the doctor?" Jack stepped closer and placed a hand on Robert's shoulder. "Are you having some sort of memory lapse again?"

"Again? No, no, I'm fine. I just forgot, is all. It's been a long day. So much has happened. I should rest a while. Everything will be great tomorrow, I'm sure of it." Robert smiled a fake smile. He didn't want Jack to think he'd lost his marbles, although he wasn't certain that he hadn't.

"Jack, why aren't you married?" Robert asked. He was guessing that if Jack was married he wouldn't be in the shop stocking the shelves at night.

Jack laughed again, "I suppose the right lady hasn't caught my attention yet."

"What about Miss Ginifer Sweetly?" Robert asked. "I think she likes you." He remembered her coming into the shop wanting Jack to walk her home, but Thomas Appleton offered when Robert said he was scared to be alone.

Jack laughed again, louder this time, "She may have had an interest in me at some point, when we were young. I'm not entirely sure. But she's married now."

"Who did she marry? I can't seem to remember his name. What was his name again?"

"His name is Thomas Appleton," Jack said, and then couldn't help frowning about it.

It was clear Jack still had feelings for Miss Ginifer. Robert decided to change the subject.

"When will Lizzy come to visit again?" Robert asked.

"Actually, she'll be here in the morning. You should get some rest before then," Jack said, and returned to stocking the shelves.

"Does Mr. Lowsley come around much?" Robert asked, then bit his lip. He wanted to know if

Mr. Lowsley had been causing any trouble for them during the past 25 years.

"Mr. Lowsley doesn't come around here much anymore. I'm not sure why," Jack said. "I figured it would have been a constant struggle for us to keep our secrets from him. I imagined him lurking about with his companions since that time you let something slip about the hourglasses in front of him. But it never happened."

Jack continued, "I'm still careful what I say around him. He's probably forgotten all about it, but we still need to be careful. We've been lucky so far, but there's no telling when our luck might run out."

Robert wiped his forehead with the back of his hand, then gulped, but remained silent.

"When Mr. Lowsley does come into the shop, he just mumbles something under his breath. He's become a brooding old man, and bitter at that," Jack said.

"I'll be off to bed now, Jack," Robert didn't know what else to say.

As Robert walked up the stairs, he thought, *Mr. Lowsley demanded I explain about the hourglasses, and even threatened my family. I wonder if Mr. Lowsley's bit-*

terness came from my never telling him? And why is it that Mr. Lowsley doesn't come around much and hasn't caused any trouble for us?

As Robert kept climbing the stairs, he looked down at the shop. It seemed smaller than before. *Everything looks smaller,* he thought. *Or maybe I'm just bigger. I feel like a giant!*

On the way to his bedroom, Robert heard muffled voices. *Mother and Father!* He thought. Robert rushed to his parents' open bedroom door and peeked in. Then he lightly knocked to get their attention.

"Hello, Robert," Emma said, adjusting herself in the winged-back chair.

His mother's hair was nearly snow white. She had wrinkled lines spread around her face and forehead. *She's old,* Robert thought. *Really, really old.*

In the bed, his father smiled. His white shaggy hair and unshaved whiskers took Robert off guard. *He's really old too,* Robert thought. *And even worse, he still looks sick! This is awful!* But Robert bit his tongue and kept his shock to himself.

"I just wanted to say goodnight," Robert said. "I'm going to bed early. I'm not feeling at all well.

I need some rest." He left and walked to his own room.

Robert fell onto the bed and buried his face in the pillow. Even the bed felt smaller. Everything was different.

I still feel like I'm 10 years old, he thought, *but I look a lot older. Everyone is older! This isn't what I wished for. I want my childhood back. What have I done?*

* * *

~

CHAPTER 17

THE BROKEN CLOCK

You can't break curiosity.

—Harry Finkle

The radiant sunshine covered Robert's eyes, letting him know it was a new day. Robert rushed to get dressed, and ate a breakfast of porridge and toast in a flash. He had things to do, and he needed to get them done quickly.

At the top of his list was paying a visit to Mr. Curry, the local clockmaker. Mr. Curry could help him fix the clock!

As Robert walked to the clock shop, the early morning scent of bacon and fresh scones wafted through the air, tickling Robert's nose. His stomach grumbled, even though he'd already eaten a hearty breakfast. The smell grew stronger as he approached the baker's shop.

Robert decided to stop in the bakery for just a moment. He peered through the large window. The individual glass panes framed the array of fresh baked foods. How could he pass up a warm scone filled with fruit, or a hot cross bun covered in sweet icing? Robert licked his lips. It all smelled good and looked delicious! He dug his hands into his pockets, searching for some coins. He smiled with delight when he opened his hand and found an adult-sized amount of money to spend. Robert decided he was going to treat himself to both a scone and a bun, and a nice cup of hot tea to wash them down.

Robert entered the bakery with a smile on his face. Everything looked the same, and he felt right at home. He patiently waited his turn in line, then took a seat at one of the small round tables.

"Robert, is that you, dear?" said a lady's voice nearby.

Robert looked up to see an elderly woman walking with a cane. He didn't recognize her; she was very old. But her voice sounded awfully familiar.

He wiped his mouth, then said "Yes, that would be me. Do I know you?"

The old woman chuckled, then took a seat at his table. "I don't think it's been that long since I've seen you, dear Robert. It's me, Miss Caroline." She laughed again.

"I'm sorry, I must not be fully awake yet. How have you been? Are you selling some of your wonderful pies to the baker today?"

Miss Caroline giggled. "I don't sell my pies to the baker anymore, dear. I live upstairs in one of his spare rooms. The least I can do is bake pies for my room and board."

"Why aren't you living in your home?" Robert asked, taking a huge bite of the fruit-filled scone.

Miss Caroline's smile turned to a frown. "You remember, don't you Robert? After my home burned to the ground, I came to stay here for a while. But my visit turned into a much longer stay than expected. This is where I live now."

Robert didn't know what to say. He thought for sure Miss Caroline would have ended up living in her home again.

"But I passed your house on the way here," Robert said. "I don't understand why you aren't living there." Robert wiped his mouth and sipped his tea.

"That isn't my home anymore, dear. It belongs to Mr. Lowsley now," Miss Caroline said.

"Mr. Lowsley?" Robert said, horrified.

"Oh yes, dear, Mr. Lowsley purchased what was left of my home and built another one in its place."

"I'm sorry, Miss Caroline," Robert said, then hung his head. *This wasn't supposed to happen,* he thought. *Miss Caroline's home should have been rebuilt for* her, *not Mr. Lowsley! And worst of all, Mr. Lowsley is now living in Finkleton!*

"What would you have to be sorry about, dear? I didn't have enough coins to build another home. What was left after the fire was nothing more than a pile of rubble. And selling what was left to Mr. Lowsley was the only option I had. It was a meager amount, that's for sure, but I'm happy living here. Oh, I could have moved to another town, but this is my home. Mother Nature controls the weather, lightning included. No point dwelling on the past. Everything happens for a reason." Miss Caroline smiled. "But wouldn't it be wonderful to turn back time and change things?"

"Turn back time? What do you mean?" Robert asked.

"Oh, never mind me, dear, I'm an old woman with wishful thinking," Miss Caroline said. She stood to leave. "I bid you have a good day, dear Robert. I hope to see you again very soon." Miss Caroline winked at him before walking away with the aid of her wooden cane.

Robert left the bakery and headed down the cobblestone path towards the clockmaker. He needed to get the broken clock fixed, and fast. Everything was an absolute mess. *This is like a bad dream*, he thought. *I don't belong here. I want to be 10 years old again!*

Mr. Curry's shop had been especially built away from the other buildings, alone at the edge of the path, because of how loud his shop could get, especially when his clocks tolled together at the start of each new hour.

A massive clock hung above the entry door welcoming patrons, but Robert didn't see a single passerby walk the extra distance to visit the lonely shop.

Robert had never needed to visit the clock-maker himself, although he often wondered what the inside of the shop looked like. When Robert opened the door, he immediately heard the *ticking* and *clicking* of the clocks.

Clocks ranging in all sizes and shapes—small, large, round, square—covered every space along the walls. Gigantic grandfather clocks had been placed throughout the shop like giants in a maze. They towered over Robert's head, looking down at him at every turn. He suddenly felt like a small boy again.

An array of cuckoo clocks caught Robert's attention. A sign hung on the wall above them that read "Black Forest Cuckoo Clocks." He remembered his father once telling him that cuckoo clocks from the Black Forest were all the rage in England. At the time Robert thought the Black Forest sounded like a scary place and hoped his father would never buy a cuckoo clock. Looking at them now, though, they appeared to be harmless enough, and rather charming.

"Hello there," Mr. Curry's aged voice echoed from a distance. "I'm in the back, if you can find your way."

Robert maneuvered past clocks to reach the rear of the shop. He found Mr. Curry wearing a strange contraption over his head. It held a small magnifying glass directly in front of his eyes while he worked on a pocket watch. Mr. Curry glanced up and greeted Robert with a smile. He then set aside the small tools next to the watch and removed cotton from each of his ears.

Robert stifled a giggle. The magnifying glass made Mr. Curry's eyes appear extremely large. It was the funniest thing Robert had seen in a long time. And why would he have cotton in his ears? Robert made a mental note to visit Mr. Curry more often.

Robert explained his clock was broken and asked if Mr. Curry could help with the repair.

"Oh, yes, of course," Mr. Curry said. "You can bring it by anytime. I'll take a look and see what I can do."

"No, you don't understand," Robert said. "I *can't* bring the clock to your shop. Not without anyone knowing, that is. You see, nobody knows it's broken *yet*."

Mr. Curry smiled and said, "I think I get your meaning. But I'm not sure I can help unless you bring the clock here to me or I go to the clock itself."

"I see," Robert said, rubbing his chin. "I'll see what I can do." Robert didn't actually know what to do. He couldn't possibly take the clock out of his family's shop without someone noticing. And he couldn't invite Mr. Curry into the super-secret hourglass room either.

"I don't think I've met you before this day. What's your name?" Mr. Curry asked.

"My name is Robert. Robert Finkle."

"Finkle, you say? Robert Finkle?" Mr. Curry's eyes grew larger than before. "You're related to Harry Finkle, aren't you?"

"Yes. Yes, I am."

"Why didn't you say so in the first place?" Mr. Curry abruptly stood, then scurried off through a door behind his desk. Robert had no idea why he left and where he'd gone.

Robert could hear the sounds of papers being rummaged through and things falling to the floor with a thud. He leaned to the side and tried to peer through the open door, but couldn't see any sign of Mr. Curry. A moment after the sounds stopped, though, Mr. Curry rushed back into the shop. He adjusted his spectacles and placed an old book on the desk directly in front of Robert.

"This belonged to Harry Finkle. He came to me years ago in need of clock repair, just as you have today. And he, like you, didn't want to bring the clock in question to my shop. Instead he had me purchase this book for him. It's not a repair book, but it has enough information about old clocks to help someone figure out how to fix one. He kept it for years; and studied it, I suspect, because it looks worn. A few years before his unfortunate death, however, he returned it to me. He said he had no place for it, and wanted me to hold onto it for safekeeping."

"He said his family might one day have need of it," Mr. Curry added, and laughed.

"His family?"

"Yes. I thought the old geezer had lost his mind. His shop is ten times the size of mine, and he said he didn't have a place for it! At least he was right about one thing," Mr. Curry said.

"What?"

"You're his family, and you're here asking about clock repair." Mr. Curry laughed again.

"What's so funny?"

"I'm sorry, Robert." Mr. Curry wiped his eyes. "But how could he possibly know any of his family would have the need for clock repair? If I didn't know any better, I'd swear he'd seen the future."

"Why would you say that?" Robert gasped.

"Well, you're here, aren't you? Just as Harry thought you would be." Mr. Curry laughed again. "Here you go, Robert. This book belonged to Harry, and now it belongs to you. No need to return it. I only hope you can find a place for it!" Mr. Curry continued to laugh.

"Thank you," Robert said, taking the book from Mr. Curry.

"If you need any help, feel free to stop by. I'm always here. Have a good day." Mr. Curry shook Robert's hand, then placed the cotton back in his ears and returned to work on the pocket watch.

Robert left the shop with the book in hand—and a lot of questions. *Did my Uncle Harry travel to the future like I did?* he wondered. *And if so, was it by accident or on purpose? And did Uncle Harry truly know that I'd be needing this clock repair book?*

Robert's thoughts were interrupted by the increasingly earsplitting sounds of the clocks inside Mr. Curry's shop. If Robert had remained inside a little while longer, he would have needed cotton for his ears too.

Robert started to walk home, wondering if he would be able to fix the clock by himself.

* * *

~

CHAPTER 18

TOGETHER AGAIN

*You never truly grow up, although
your age declares differently.*

—Harry Finkle

Robert went straight back home. He noticed Jack behind the counter writing in the shop ledger. It was Robert's job to log the supplies in the ledger, and he'd assumed that he would always be the one to do so. *It's odd what changes with time,* he thought.

"Hello, Robert," Jack greeted him, smiling. "Did you enjoy visiting the bakery today?"

"How did you know I went to the bakery?" Robert's voice squeaked.

Jack laughed. "You are forever visiting the bakery. Where else would you go?"

"You're right." Robert laughed along. It felt good to know some things would never change. He'd have to go back later and purchase a fruit-filled scone for Jack...and maybe another one for himself.

Robert returned to the hourglass room. He placed the book Mr. Curry had given him on the desk and casually flipped through the pages. There was a lot of technical information. He decided to read it later that evening, after the shop closed for the day. It would be better to have no distractions.

Just outside the storage room entrance leading to the shop, Robert overheard Jack and a lady speaking in hushed tones. He strained to hear them but couldn't make out what they were saying.

Robert stepped into the shop to see Jack speaking to a petite blonde woman, with her hair pulled back at the nape of her neck. A strand of her curly hair had fallen forward during the conversation.

He heard them speaking of someone needing to take care of parents and Robert. She pushed the tendril behind her ear, then smiled when she noticed Robert standing in the doorway.

"Good morning, Robert," the lady said. Her voice sounded familiar, and her features resembled someone he knew. Exactly who that was hit him like a thunderbolt. This lady was none other than his sister, Lizzy!

"Hello!" Robert replied in astonishment. He tried to speak again, but stumbled on his words. He could barely believe he was seeing Lizzy all grown up.

"You appear to be more alert today, Robert," Lizzy said.

"What do you mean by that?" Robert asked. Jack leaned his elbow on the counter and did not dare interrupt.

"It's just that you seem more *awake* than usual," Lizzy said, smiling. "And that's a good thing. Wouldn't you agree?"

"I overheard you talking," Robert said.

"You were eavesdropping!" Lizzy said disapprovingly.

"No, I was listening, and you just didn't happen to notice. I wasn't being secretive about it. Huge difference, if you ask me."

Jack stifled a giggle with a low cough to clear his throat. Robert grinned. Lizzy had said something very similar to him years ago. It felt good to turn the tables on her. No matter how old Robert got, he would always enjoy getting a rise out of his sister. Lizzy glared at Jack, and then at Robert.

"And why would anyone need to take care of me? I'm not 10 years old anymore, as you can very well see," Robert said.

"Well," Lizzy said, and dropped her eyes to the floor for a moment. "It's just that you've been in a kind of daze since Father's accident. You've been not at all yourself for many years."

"Robert," Jack interjected, "what Lizzy is trying to say is that you've been here, but you really haven't been here, if that makes any sense."

"No, it doesn't make sense at all. You're both talking in circles. You don't have to take care of me. I'm all grown up," Robert said, growing angrier with each word. "When will you stop treating me like a child?" Robert's hands balled into fists. He dashed out of the shop.

Robert was horrified that after so many years Jack and Lizzy still considered him a little boy. *Apparently some things will never change!* he thought.

After all, I'm not 10 years old anymore. Well, actually I am—but they don't know that! And what do they mean, I've been here but not here? They're not making any sense. Maybe they've *lost* their *marbles!*

Robert stormed into the hourglass room and slammed the door behind him, then walked over to the desk and sat down on the wooden chair.

What am I going to do? He wondered. Everything is wrong! It isn't fair! Robert sat in silence for a moment, then opened the bottom drawer of the desk drawers. After 25 years, it was still where he'd left it: the *Book of Memories.* He picked up the book and placed it on the desk, then opened it to reveal the mysterious blank pages.

I don't understand why Miss Caroline sold her home to Mr. Lowsley. Surly she could have had the means to live on her own with her famous pies and save enough coins to rebuild. It wasn't like she was under any pressure to sell to that vicious man. Robert placed a hand on one of the blank pages. "Why would Miss Caroline sell her home to Mr. Lowsley? Why would she accept a meager amount? Help me understand."

Letters began to appear on the blank page, swirling until the words formed complete sentences. The *Book of Memories* explained the terms set forth by Miss Caroline, which were reluctantly accepted by Mr. Lowsley.

Mr. Lowsley offered Miss Caroline a generous price for her property. In fact, it was such an enormous amount that she would have been able to move to another town and live a very comfortable life. Mr. Lowsley was shocked to learn that she wanted something beyond money.

Miss Caroline decided she would sell her property to Mr. Lowsley only if he agreed to some unusual conditions. After Miss Caroline explained her terms, Mr. Lowsley demanded her to accept a significantly reduced price for her property. The conditions in the contract read as followed:

First, Mr. Lowsley promises to always maintain a distance from Jack, Lizzy and Robert. Outside of earshot wasn't far enough, it had to be much farther than that. A distance of 200 cobblestones would be enough to satisfy this agreement.

Second, Mr. Lowsley promises to not enter the Finkle's shop without Miss Caroline or someone of her choosing being there. He would only be allowed to speak to Jack, Lizzy or Robert while making a purchase.

Third, Mr. Lowsley's companions must also abide by the same rules set forth in the agreement.

Fourth, In the event Mr. Lowsley or his companions ever violate the agreement, ownership of the land and any new home built, will immediately revert to Miss Caroline. In addition Miss Caroline would be able to keep the money Mr. Lowsley paid her to purchase the property.

Fifth, Mr. Lowsley was not allowed to repeat the conditions of the contract to anyone, including his companions.

Robert sat in silence, taking it all in. *Miss Caroline sacrificed her home to keep us all safe from Mr. Lowsley. Why would she do that?* Robert wondered. *It definitely explains why Mr. Lowsley hasn't caused any more trouble during the past 25 years.* Robert placed the book back into the desk drawer, then adjusted his spectacles.

I need to fix things as soon as possible, and the only way is to figure out how to repair the clock! From this moment forward, I won't stop until I make things right. Robert snatched up the book Mr. Curry gave him and examined the pages more carefully.

Robert quickly realized he didn't know enough about the clock yet to decide where to begin reading. He set the book back on the desk and reached above the desk to remove the clock from the wall. He would need to open the clock and inspect it first.

Just as Robert placed his hands on the clock, though, the door opened. He turned to see Jack and Lizzy standing in the doorway with their mouths open. Lizzy gasped, then covered her mouth.

"What do you think you're doing, Robert?" Jack yelled. "Leave the clock alone! We all agreed to *never* touch that clock!"

"Please let go of the clock, Robert," Lizzy pleaded in a calmer voice than Jack.

"I'm a grown man!" Robert yelled. "Stop telling me what to do!"

"Robert, please," Lizzy said, entering the room. "I'm not telling you what to do. But we cannot touch that clock. We don't know what it's capable of doing. Something could go horribly wrong!"

"Something already has gone wrong." Robert let go of the clock and picked up its broken pieces. He showed them the broken parts resting on his palm.

"Robert, what have you done?" Lizzy said accusingly.

Robert ignored Lizzy and looked at Jack. "Can you help me fix it?" Robert pleaded. "I need your help. I can't do this by myself, but you can fix anything. You fixed the lever under the counter when it was broken."

Jack solemnly inspected the mechanical fragments in Robert's hand. "Repairing the clock will take some time. I would need to reassemble the pieces to be sure."

Robert hung his head, then said in almost a whisper, "I must return."

Jack looked at Robert in puzzlement. "Return where, Robert?"

"Finkleton!" Robert said with his newfound voice.

Jack laughed, "What are you going on about now, Robert? You've never left Finkleton."

"I must return to Finkleton. The Finkleton I once knew!" Robert roared.

"It's the heat, I just know it," Lizzy said. "Maybe you should see the doctor."

"It's not the heat, Lizzy!" Robert raised his voice again.

"What is it then?" she asked.

* * *

~

CHAPTER 19

TIME TO EXPLAIN

The truth is sometimes hard to believe.

—Harry Finkle

Robert felt the walls closing in on him. The room started to spin. He placed a hand on the back of the chair to steady himself. It was indeed time to explain. He needed to tell Jack and Lizzy everything. If he wanted to ever be 10 years old again, he needed Jack's help to fix the clock.

Robert told them about the fire, Miss Caroline's home, their father's accident, and Mr. Lowsley overhearing him talk about the hourglasses.

"We already know about those things, Robert. What do they have to do with this clock?" Lizzy asked impatiently.

Robert ignored Lizzy's complaint and continued to explain. He told them how he turned the hands of the clock and that he didn't think it worked, but then the clock broke. And here he was 25 years older than last week.

Jack scratched his head, taking in everything Robert had said, but not showing if he believed him or not. Lizzy, on the other hand, giggled and shook her head, then placed a hand on her forehead in disbelief.

"You seem a bit tired, Robert. Maybe you should go upstairs and lay down for a while. I'm sure you'll feel better in the morning. You'll see," Lizzy said, smiling at Robert as if he were a small pet that needed calming.

"Stop treating me like I'm a child, Lizzy!" Robert yelled. "I'm a grown man in front of your very eyes!"

Lizzy was taken aback by Robert's sudden outburst. "I only meant for you to get some rest, Robert." Lizzy's eyes lowered with worry.

Robert needed help with the clock. He paced the floor thinking. Jack and Lizzy didn't believe a word he said. He had to try harder. What could he say to make them believe what he told them?

Suddenly it came to him. Robert stopped pacing the floor. "I know about the secret room beneath the floor in the library!"

Jack and Lizzy awakened from their stupor. Lizzy gasped and grabbed the chair to steady herself. Jack crossed his arms over his chest.

"You know about the hidden room? How and when did you find it?" Lizzy asked.

"You never knew I'd returned from helping Miss Caroline," Robert said. "I stood outside the door and heard you talking about the hidden room."

Jack and Lizzy were silent. They were hanging on every word Robert was saying. Curiosity, grief and panic crossed their faces. Robert continued to pace the floor.

"And I know about the glowing book! I'd thought we were done keeping secrets, but I guess I was wrong about that. It's been 25 years since you found the hidden room! Why didn't you tell me?" Robert asked. Neither Jack nor Lizzy answered him.

Robert was enraged. He turned to Jack. "And you never told us about Mr. Lowsley!"

"What about Mr. Lowsley?"

"It was the day I mentioned the hourglasses in front of Miss Caroline and Mr. Lowsley. It was the day you followed him to find out if he suspected anything." Robert was furious. Jack didn't say a word.

"What do you mean, Robert?" Lizzy asked, looking at Jack in disbelief. "Jack, you said you didn't find Mr. Lowsley. What is Robert talking about?"

"He found him, all right!" Robert exclaimed. He told them of the conversation Mr. Lowsley had with his two companions while Jack hid behind the feed sacks.

"How do you know of these things, Robert?" Jack's voice boomed through the room. "Tell me!" he demanded. "How do you know?"

"When I searched the hidden room you and Lizzy spoke of, there were a bunch of books on the desk. On the bottom was one titled *Book of Memories*. The pages were blank, but when I asked a question letters appeared out of nowhere that answered whatever I wanted to know."

"The book sound fascinating," Lizzy said. "Although it's hard to believe. And where might this book be now?"

Jack interrupted. "This all sounds a bit far-fetched if you ask me, Robert. But what you say about the secret room and Mr. Lowsley is true enough."

Robert next told them about Mr. Lowsley cornering him and demanding information. "I was too afraid to tell you, and besides Mr. Lowsley threatened to hurt our whole family if I said anything to anyone. What was I supposed to do?" Robert hung his head.

"Mr. Lowsley was just bluffing, Robert. He never would have followed through with his threats. It was his way of trying to get answers out of you. Do you really think I'd let anything happen to you? I'll always be here for you, Robert. You should never be afraid of telling me anything," Jack said.

Robert then began to explain about the glowing book he discovered. He told them of the secret lever, just like the one under the counter in the shop that controls the rain.

Robert lowered his eyes when he told them of pulling the lever hidden behind the book titled *Lightning*. His voice began to squeak when he told them of lightning striking precisely at that moment, of how loud the sounds were and how he became scared.

Robert wiped away a tear that rolled down his cheek before saying, "Father is sick because of me, and Miss Caroline's home burned because of me. It's my entire fault! And now Mr. Lowsley owns her property. He finally got what he wanted! You have to believe me!" Robert slammed his fist on the desk.

"Show us the book," Lizzy said.

"What?" Robert replied.

"Show us the *Book of Memories*. If everything you say is true, then show us the book and prove it to us," Lizzy said.

"Fine." Robert opened the bottom drawer of the desk and removed the book once again. He picked it up and placed it on the desk for them to see.

Lizzy slid her hand down the front cover. "It's quite old."

"Yes, it is," Robert said. "Now I'll prove what I've been telling you. Don't say anything, I'll do the talking."

Robert opened the book to reveal the empty pages. He touched a page, just as he did before, then asked "Who is to blame for Miss Caroline's home catching fire?"

All of a sudden letters began to appear on the page in a swirling motion. Lizzy gasped and covered her mouth. Jack just watched with great interest, bending down to more closely examine the peculiar book. The swirling letters finally revealed the answer.

"Lewis Lowsley," the book wrote.

"What?" Robert exclaimed. He removed his hand from the page. "That's not true! I caused the fire! I pulled the lightning lever!"

He placed his hand back onto the page, "How is this possible? You aren't making any sense!"

On the opposite page, lines began to appear in different directions. All at once it turned into a sketch. The drawing showed lightning high in the sky, but not once did the bolts touch the ground or any buildings.

The next drawing revealed Mr. Lowsley and his two companions, Peter and Paul, just outside of Miss Caroline's home. They had wrapped scraps of cloth around the ends of several small sticks. Mr. Lowsley lit them on fire, and then the three of them threw the fiery sticks up high enough for them to land on the thatched roof. A blazing fire could be seen in no time.

"I thought I caused the fire, but it all makes perfect sense now," Robert said. "When I looked out the shop window and saw Miss Caroline's home on fire, Mr. Lowsley and his companions were talking. He told them the lightning created the perfect opportunity to finally purchase a home in Finkleton. It was them that started the fire. The book doesn't lie!"

A look of sorrow crossed Lizzy's face. Her lips parted as if she wanted to say something, but couldn't find the words.

"We're sorry, Robert. We didn't know," Jack said as he stepped closer to Robert and placed a hand on his shoulder.

"All this time, I thought it was me that caused the fire. Do you have any idea how that felt? And it was always Mr. Lowsley!" Robert turned to his brother. "Will you help me, Jack? Will you help me fix the clock?"

"Yes, yes, of course, Robert," Jack said. He squeezed his younger brother's shoulder. "It'll be like old times. Something breaks and I fix it. But usually I'm the one who breaks it!" Jack and Robert both laughed.

The brothers carefully removed the clock from the wall, making sure to not to lose any more pieces or damage the string that was attached.

Robert decided to tell Jack and Lizzy about the contract between Miss Caroline and Mr. Lowsley, and how she allowed her land to be sold for much less than it was worth.

"Sounds like she really had our best interests at heart," Lizzy said. "She's a wonderful lady. Fortunately, she's very happy living with the Baker's. And she gets to bake her wonderful pies every day."

"But why would she give up living a good life?" Robert asked. "It doesn't make any sense. Why would Miss Caroline give up all that money just to make sure Mr. Lowsley kept his distance from us?"

"Maybe she was fond of Uncle Harry," Jack suggested.

"Miss Caroline obviously doesn't want us to know, since she hasn't mentioned anything about it in all these years," Lizzy said. "I think we should leave it alone. No point being nosey and bringing up the past."

Lizzy began to read the book that Mr. Curry gave to Robert. She turned each page in search of information about repairing their particular clock. "I wonder how Uncle Harry realized that we would one day be in need of this book," Lizzy wondered out loud.

Jack and Robert shrugged. "We may never know," Jack said.

Lizzy kept reading, and then smiled. "Uncle Harry scribbled the strangest thoughts in the most unexpected of places."

"What do you mean, Lizzy?" Jack asked.

"This is what Uncle Harry wrote across the top of a page of the book: 'One day my shop will be decorated with a multitude of colors resembling a display of spring flowers.'"

"That *is* a bit strange," Jack said. "It doesn't make any sense, in my opinion. Were those really his hopes for the shop?" Lizzy shrugged and kept reading.

Jack, Robert and Lizzy continued to examine the clock and the book well into the evening. Lizzy left the hourglass room several times to help patrons entering the shop, announced by the bell hanging over the entry door.

Finally Jack stood and stretched his back. "It's getting rather late, Robert. I'm afraid I won't be of much good for the rest of the night. We can finish up in the morning. One more night won't hurt."

"I think it best I stay overnight," Lizzy said. "Finian won't mind, and I'm sure the children are fast asleep by now. I'll sleep in my old room. See you in the morning. Goodnight, Jack. Goodnight, Robert."

Robert's mind was set at ease. Jack and Lizzy were helping him fix the clock. He was going to return to where he belonged. He couldn't wait to be 10 years old again.

Robert stretched, then followed Jack up the stairs. "It has been a long day."

"Tomorrow will be better, Robert," Jack said. "You'll see."

Robert could hardly wait. He was going to go home. And he was going to make things right.

* * *

~

CHAPTER 20

A STRANGER VISITS
THE SHOP

Trust your eyes, for they see more than you do.

—Harry Finkle

Robert slept late. His stomach rumbled from missing breakfast. He snatched up a piece of cold dry toast and thought he could probably spare a moment to visit the bakery and fill his belly. He was so hungry he knew he could eat at least five fruit-filled scones all by himself.

Coming down the stairs, Robert stopped when he noticed Lizzy unrolling spools of different colored ribbons. It made him giggle, because they were longer than she was tall. She held an end piece of ribbon, then rolled the spool on the floor to allow the ribbon to uncoil. Pleased with the result, she grabbed two spools at once and unrolled them the same way.

Lizzy then wrapped the ribbons around tall bolsters of fabric set upright on a round table in the center of the shop. Lizzy weaved the ribbons through the handles of shears, then used pincushions to hold them in place. The entire display looked like a huge gift wrapped in delicate ribbons. The different shades of colors were eye–popping, and a pleasing distraction. Lizzy stepped back to admire her work, and smiled. "They brighten up the old place, don't you think?"

Jack examined the display from behind the counter. "You've outdone yourself, Lizzy," Jack said, and clapped to applaud her work.

Lizzy curtsied. "Thank you, Jack! It's nice that you still appreciate me after all these years. Perhaps I can do something with the baking supplies as well." They both laughed.

Lizzy turned and noticed Robert at the bottom of the stairs. "Good morning, Robert," she said, smiling.

"Good morning, Lizzy, Jack," Robert said, and nodded his head. "Are we going to work on the clock anytime soon?"

"Yes, of course. I just want to finish taking inventory, if you don't mind. I need to place an order with a few of the farmers this afternoon. I was supposed to have it finished yesterday, but time got away from me," Jack said, chuckling.

"I'll give you a hand, Jack," Robert said as he approached the front of the counter. Jack slid the ledger in front of him. "It's nice to know I'll still be needed when I turn 35," Robert said.

"You'll always be needed, no matter what your age is, Robert," Jack said.

It was nearly noon by the time the inventory and order had been completed. Jack and Robert mentioned food several times, but Lizzy took no notice. Then she began feeling a bit famished herself.

"I'll fetch us a few sandwiches to tide us over until tea," Lizzy announced, wiping her hands on a small towel.

Before Lizzy could step out from behind the counter, however, the shop bell chimed again. Two well-dressed gentlemen in their mid-20s entered.

They began browsing the shop, keeping to themselves.

Jack and Robert now had to work in the shop to avoid raising any customer suspicion. Jack started arranging large tins filled with flour in a complete circle on one of the round tables in the center of the room. With Robert's help he then placed medium-sized tins of baking ingredients on top of the large tins. The brothers also tied some extra ribbon around a dozen long wooden spoons and hung them to dangle from the edges of the table. The result was a visually appealing new baking supplies display consisting of tins filled with flour, sugar, cocoa, and cinnamon.

The gentlemen seemed to be well-pleased, although curious about the new display created right in front of them in a matter of minutes. They pointed to a few of the other displays and made comments about the overall cleanliness of the shop. They also admired the recently-painted walls, the see-thru windows free of grime, the well-kept floor, and the extent of the inventory.

At one point Jack overheard them whisper, "Everything looks the same, just better somehow."

Jack didn't know who these men were, but they seemed a bit too curious and nosey. He decided to find out more. "Hello, gentleman. Can we be of any assistance to you today?"

The taller man said, "No, I believe we're doing just fine. Thank you for asking." The man smiled, then turned to his companion and continued to talk in low whispers.

Jack wasn't ready to give up that easily. "I don't believe we've met before. Are you new in town?"

"No, we've lived here all our lives," the taller man replied. "We just don't come around often. May I ask your names?"

"I'm Jack, and this is my sister Lizzy." Lizzy nodded her head. "And this is our brother Robert." Robert also nodded.

"Do you own this fine shop?" the taller man asked.

"Actually, our parents do. They inherited it from my father's uncle, after his passing," Jack said.

The taller man's eyes widened in alarm. He took a step back to absorb the information. The shorter gentlemen took hold of his elbow to prevent him from bumping into one of the displays.

After steadying himself, the taller man asked, "Might I be so bold as to ask when this unfortunate event happened?"

The shorter man nudged the taller man in his side and interrupted the conversation before Jack could respond. "I'm sorry, my companion tends to ask too many questions that do not concern him." He gave the taller gentlemen a look demanding that be the end of it.

"Yes, yes, please forgive my rudeness. I am truly sorry for your family's loss." The taller man dipped his eyes and nodded to Jack for acceptance.

The shorter man asked the next question: "Where is your father, by the way?"

"He's upstairs in bed. Mother is tending to him. He took ill after the accident. We've run the shop by ourselves since we were young," Jack replied.

"Accident, you say?" The shorter man looked genuinely concerned. "I'm sorry to hear that. Please wish your father well for me. And how has the weather been in Finkleton?"

Before Jack could respond, this time the taller man interrupted. "Everything looks to be in good order, and I must say you've done a fine job running the shop. You don't seem to have any trouble with the fairies, I see."

"Fairies?" Lizzy's voice squeaked. "What do you mean, fairies?"

The taller man laughed. "I take it you don't believe in them?"

"No one in their right mind believes in fairies!" Lizzy exclaimed.

"Well, I do," he said. "One of the fairies that dwells in my home is a messy one. He enjoys causing me trouble and peeling the paint off the walls. I wouldn't wish him on anyone." The man smiled. "His family isn't so bad, though."

"What's his name? The fairy, that is," Lizzy clarified.

"I call him Bob," he said, and laughed under his breath. "He has a much longer name, but I enjoy irritating him as much as he does me. So Bob it is."

These gentlemen are beginning to sound a bit too curious, Robert thought. *They've commented on the shop and asked about the weather, and now they're talking about silly fairies.* "You've lived in Finkleton your entire lives?" Robert asked.

"Yes, but time changes everything, I'm afraid. It's a funny thing, time that is," the taller gentleman said.

"What's funny about time?" Robert asked defensively.

"Robert!" Lizzy scolded.

The taller man laughed. "Please excuse me. I'm talking nonsense. But if I could control time, I might change a few things. Again, I must apologize. We really must be getting back." He looked at Robert, then said "Our future depends on it." And he winked.

Neither Jack nor Lizzy saw the man wink at Robert. *That was very peculiar, to say the least,* Robert thought.

"Keep up the great work. It was very nice to meet you all," the taller man said. He and his companion turned to leave.

The taller man glanced back once more before walking through the door and waved his hand towards Lizzy's new display, "Might I also say, your centerpiece is quite lovely. It reminds me of a fresh bouquet of spring flowers. Again, it was very nice to meet you all."

Jack nodded. "And you as well, Mr.—?"

The taller man replied, "You may call me Harry. And this is George. Have a *wonderful* afternoon." Both gentlemen smiled, then quietly took their leave without saying another word.

* * *

∽

CHAPTER 21

MISS CAROLINE AND THE GHOST

The past will visit you in the future.

—Harry Finkle

J ack, Lizzy and Robert all stood with their mouths hanging open. What was that strange conversation with those unusually curious men all about?

Breaking the silence, the shop bell rang again to announce another patron. Jack, Lizzy and Robert all peered around to see who had entered.

Miss Caroline stood ashen in the doorway. Her hands were shaking, and her face had lost all color. Lizzy rushed to her side.

"Miss Caroline! Miss Caroline! Please sit down." Lizzy guided Miss Caroline to a small table in front of the largest window.

"I'll get you something to drink, shall I?" Lizzy didn't wait for an answer. She rushed over a pitcher of water, filled a glass and put it on the table. Miss Caroline sat silent for a moment, then reached for the glass and took a small sip.

"Are you all right, Miss Caroline?" Lizzy asked. Jack and Robert hovered close by in case their help was needed.

"I think I've just seen a ghost. Actually, two ghosts!" Miss Caroline said. She took another sip of water, trying to hold the glass steady.

"A ghost?" Jack asked.

"During the day? Not possible," Robert said, rolling his eyes. Jack nudged him to be quiet.

"Yes, a ghost. Two of them! I noticed Mr. Lowsley down the way, and I decided to pop in and visit you for just a moment. He's been relentless about purchasing more property in Finkleton."

"But what about the ghosts?" Lizzy pressed. "Who do you think you saw?"

Miss Caroline took Lizzy's hand. "I would wager my best pie that I have just seen your Great Uncle Harry and his brother—your Grandfather George—walking out of your shop."

Lizzy gasped.

"They looked dashingly young, but I remember them clearly," Miss Caroline said. "My mind is still sharp as an eagle. I'll always remember what those two look like."

She waved her hand in the air and took another sip of water. "Never mind me, dears. I'm getting old. Maybe my eyes are playing tricks on me. I really must be on my way." Miss Caroline left the shop as quick as she came.

As soon as Miss Caroline was gone, Robert bolted towards the stairs, with Jack and Lizzy hot on his heels. "What was Grandfather's first name?" Robert asked as he climbed the steps.

"I can't remember!" Lizzy said, clearly out of breath as they reached the top.

"Let's calm down and think about this for just a moment," Jack said, leaning against the wall. "This is too much excitement for one day. It can't be possible. It just can't be."

"What do you mean it can't be possible?" Robert asked. "I'm here, aren't I?"

"It's true, Jack. Anything is possible," Lizzy said. "But let's not jump to any conclusions. We can ask Mother and Father. That should settle this."

"You're right, Lizzy," Jack said. "Shall we?"

Jack, Lizzy and Robert quietly stood outside their parents' bedroom listening. Robert lightly knocked on the door.

"Come in, come in," Emma said invitingly.

They gathered in the room at the foot of their parents' bed. Emma was seated in the winged-back chair at the side of the bed holding her husband's hand. William appeared to be sleeping.

"What is it, children?" Emma asked.

"Mother," Lizzy began, "what is Grandfather's first name on Father's side?"

"Why do you ask, dear?"

"We're just curious, Mother," Robert said.

At that moment William coughed and opened his eyes. "Hello, children."

"Oh, Father. We didn't mean to wake you. We're sorry. We'll leave now." Lizzy lowered her eyes.

"You're not bothering me, children. It's always a pleasure to see you," William said in a weak, raspy voice. "I may not have ever mentioned my father's name. I'm sorry for that. My father's name was George."

* * *

∾

CHAPTER 22

TIME TO FIX TIME

Remember your future when visiting the past.

— Harry Finkle

ack, Lizzy and Robert rushed to the hourglass room before beginning to speak.

"It must have been Great Uncle Harry and Grandfather George when they were young!" Lizzy said. "But what I don't understand is how they came to the future and *remained* young!"

"What do you mean, Lizzy?" Jack asked.

"Look at Robert! He's not young. He's 35 years old. Just look at him," Lizzy said, appraising her brother. "Take no offense, Robert."

"I'm not old, Lizzy. I'm 10," Robert pointed out.

"Exactly! And yet you appear to be 35. So why didn't Uncle Harry and Grandfather George also look decades older?"

"You've got a good point, Lizzy," Jack agreed.

"I don't know why," Robert said. "But I need to find out!"

"Don't you think you've caused enough trouble, Robert?" Lizzy pointed a finger at his chest. "I don't mean to be rude by saying this, but meddling around with such things could in fact cause more problems."

"I suppose you're right," Robert said, hanging his head.

"When you return to Finkleton—the Finkleton you know, that is—you must tell the young versions of Jack and me *everything*. Then we'll be able find out what's going on together." Lizzy smiled. "It'll be a new adventure!"

"That sounds like a fine idea." Robert beamed with joy. "I will, I promise."

"It's time to fix this clock," Jack said, stepping over to the desk. "If those men are who we think they are, then Robert will be able to go back to where he belongs."

"Yes, I agree," Robert said. "It's time to fix the clock."

The hours passed as Jack, Robert and Lizzy worked together on the repair. It grew dark outside, and they all became tired. Lizzy dozed off in a chair with the book laying open on her lap.

Finally, Jack proclaimed "It's done!"

Lizzy woke from her nap. "What's that?"

"The clock is fixed," Jack said proudly.

"You've done it, Jack!" Robert said.

Jack and Robert hung the clock back on the wall above the desk. "Are you sure you know what you're doing, Robert?" Jack asked.

"Yes, I do. I'll fix everything back in my time. Father, Miss Caroline's home, Mr. Lowsley, and you," Robert said, placing a hand on Jack's shoulder.

"Me? What do you have to fix with me?" Jack asked.

Robert laughed, then stepped next to the chair. "You'll see, Jack. Trust me."

Jack laughed too. "All right, Robert. I do trust you. Just be careful. And remember—I'll always be here for you, no matter what happens."

"I know, Jack," Robert said, then wiped a stray tear from his eye.

"One more thing, Robert," Jack said. "If for some reason you can't change things, promise that you'll come tell me and Lizzy about Mr. Lowsley's questions and threats. We won't let anything happen to you. There's no need for you to be afraid."

"I promise, Jack," Robert said.

"I wonder if we'll know if you fixed everything. When you get back, that is," Lizzy said, worried.

"I don't think you will. But don't worry, I can do this. Trust me," Robert said.

"I do, Robert," Lizzy said, and hugged him. "Oh, and one more thing. I'm sorry I nagged you so much when we were children. I didn't mean to be annoying."

Robert laughed. "You weren't that bad, Lizzy. I learned a lot from you and your books. Besides, I enjoyed driving you insane."

Jack, Lizzy and Robert laughed together. Robert then stood on the chair directly in front of the clock. He turned to look at Jack and Lizzy once more.

Jack winked at Robert, and Lizzy smiled. Then they left the hourglass room, closing the door quietly behind them. *I'm going to miss the older Jack and Lizzy,* Robert thought. *But I'll see them again. I'll grow up with them and grow older with them.*

Robert looked at the clock hanging on the wall. Everything was quiet except for the clock going *tick tock, tick tock.*

Robert knew it was time to return to his time.

* * *

~

CHAPTER 23

RETURN TO FINKLETON

Finding your way home can be a bit tricky.

— Harry Finkle

obert cautiously reached for the clock. He placed one hand on the edge of it and the other on the small hour hand. *This is it,* he thought.

Robert began turning the hour hand counterclockwise. He didn't want to turn the hand too fast for fear of breaking it again. But Robert was eager to get the job done, just the same.

Round and round he turned the hand. *How many times did I turn the hand before?* he wondered. *I don't want to go back too far.*

Robert carefully let go of the clock hand, then stepped down from the chair. The room seemed bigger, and he felt smaller. Had he returned?

Robert bolted from the hourglass room into the shop, rushed up the stairs, and stood outside his parents' bedroom. The door was open. He saw his mother asleep in the winged-back chair and his father ill in bed. Both were the age they were supposed to be.

I made it back! Robert thought. *I must be 10 years old again.*

For a moment, Robert rejoiced. And then he thought some more. *I didn't make anything better! Everything is just as awful as when I left. Father is still sick in bed. And that means Miss Caroline's home is also still gone. I haven't fixed anything.*

Robert returned to the hourglass room. He stood upon the chair once again. *I need to go back further,* he thought. *I must make things right.*

Robert reached for the small clock hand again and began turning it slowly. He still couldn't remember how many times he'd turned it the first time. *I don't want to go back too far,* he thought. *I wouldn't want to run into Uncle Finkle and have to confess the mess I made. Nor do I want to end up being 2 years old and too little to turn the clock's hands forward.*

With that thought, Robert let go of the hour hand. He suddenly felt dizzy. The room was spinning. He placed his hands on the wall to keep himself from falling off the chair. When the room felt right again, Robert let go of the wall and stepped down from the chair.

Robert still felt like he was 10 years old. With great hope he left the hourglass room and burst into the shop.

Lizzy was sitting at the small table in front of the large window with Miss Caroline. Both of them were their normal ages. Robert was thrilled!

"Lizzy! Have you met Fin yet?" Robert asked. He hated to interrupt, but he had to know.

"Who?" Lizzy replied.

"You know, Finian Beanly. Fin! Have you met him yet?"

"You're talking in circles, Robert. I don't have the foggiest idea who you're referring to," Lizzy said. She waved her hand in the air to end Robert's rant.

"Oh, how time flies, Robert," Miss Caroline said sweetly. "I haven't seen much of you lately."

"I've been a little busy," Robert said. He tried to act normal, but fidgeted with his hands.

Miss Caroline folded her hands in her lap. "You should consider slowing down a bit. A little more time would do the trick, I should think."

"Yes, Miss Caroline," Robert said, and turned to leave. Before walking into the storage room, he glanced towards Miss Caroline. Curiously, she was staring back at him. She winked, then smiled as he left the shop. *Does she know?* Robert wondered. *How could she? It's not possible.*

Robert paused on the other side of the door opening, and quietly listened to Lizzy's and Miss Caroline's conversation.

"Miss Caroline?"

"Yes, dear," Miss Caroline said, turning to bring her full attention back to Lizzy.

"You know everyone in Finkleton. Who is Finian Beanly?"

"He's Mr. Simon Beanly's only son. His mother died during childbirth, and Mr. Beanly has raised him by himself. I don't see much of him, but he seems to be a good-hearted young man." Miss Caroline smiled and sipped her tea.

Robert quietly giggled. *Lizzy is such a girl,* he thought. *But then again, she* will *marry Finian Beanly when she gets older. I wonder if I should tell her?* He considered a moment. *No. I should keep my meddling to a minimum, and just pay attention to fixing things.*

Robert crept back to the hourglass room and stood upon the chair once more. *Did Miss Caroline really know anything?* he wondered.

"Consider slowing down a bit. A little more time would do the trick," Robert whispered, repeating what Miss Caroline had said to him.

Robert placed his finger on the small clock hand. He only needed to go back a little further. Not too much! He turned the hand round and round. He watched the hour hand and tried his best to figure out how many more hours he needed to go back. Finally he let go.

Robert felt dizzy again. He steadied himself until the room stopped spinning, then stepped down from the chair. He took a deep breath before leaving the hourglass room. *I hope that's the last time I have to use the clock,* he thought. *I hope I'm back where I belong, before everything bad happened.*

* * *

CHAPTER 24

MISS GINIFER SWEETLY

*Take advantage of an opportunity
when it presents itself.
You may not get another chance.*

—Harry Finkle

R obert held his breath as he entered the large room of the general shop. He noticed Jack balancing on a shaky three-legged stool.

Robert muffled a giggle, then asked, "What are you doing, Jack?" *Did I go back far enough?* Robert wondered. *Jack stocks the shelves all the time.*

"I'm restocking the shelves, like I always do at the end of the day," Jack said. Jack placed a few tins on the top shelf and straightened them one by one.

"Have you finished your inspection of the hourglasses and decided to finally come help me?" Jack asked. "Hand me another tin, will you please?"

"Here you go, Jack," Robert said, and handed his brother a tin. But inwardly, Robert rejoiced. *I remember this!* he thought. *I'm back when I belong!*

Just then the shop bell hanging above the entrance door rang. A young lady carrying a small package entered and carefully scanned the store. When she spotted Jack and Robert at the back, she smiled.

Jack stepped down from the stool and wiped his hands on his trousers. "Hello, Miss Ginifer. How are you this evening?"

This is it! Robert thought excitedly. *This is where it all started. This is when my first mistake happened! Now I can make everything right, starting with Jack.* Robert listened intently. He didn't want to miss his chance.

"I'm quite well, thank you for asking, Jack," Miss Ginifer replied. "I've brought your order," she said, and stepped forward to hand over the package.

Just then the shop bell rang once again. Thomas Appleton stepped inside and walked over to the counter. He turned towards Jack and Robert, then tapped his fingers impatiently.

Robert narrowed his eyes. He remembered everything. *Did Thomas truly want to walk Miss Ginifer home?* he wondered. *Or had it simply been because I acted like a scared child?*

"Thank you," Jack said to Miss Ginifer. His cheeks turned a light shade of pink, and a shine of sweat appeared on his forehead.

"Would you mind very much walking me home, Jack?" Miss Ginifer asked, and smiled.

Jack cleared his throat, then looked at Robert. "Will you keep an eye on the shop while I'm gone? I won't be long."

"Me? You want *me* to watch the shop all by myself?" Robert's eyes widened. *Oh, no! I hadn't meant to respond that way! I was caught off guard because I was thinking of what happened in the past. But this is the past! It's becoming hard to keep things straight.*

"You'll be fine, Robert. You're 10 years old now, and I won't be gone long."

Robert paused and composed himself.

Then he said, "Yes, you're right, Jack. I *am* 10 years old. I won't be scared." Robert smiled. *This is it!* "Everything will be fine. You'll see!"

Thomas' laughter immediately filled the shop. Jack, Robert and Ginifer turned towards him.

Oh no, Robert thought. *Thomas is still here. It's not over yet!*

"I'm sorry. I didn't mean to interrupt your conversation," Thomas said, then coughed to stifle his outburst. "But I think I have a solution to your problem, Jack."

Jack narrowed his eyes and crossed his arms over his chest.

Robert crossed his arms over his chest too, and glared at Thomas.

"As I was saying," Thomas continued, "I could assist Robert while you walk Miss Ginifer home. I need to purchase some supplies and he wouldn't be left alone."

Miss Ginifer looked at Jack and waited for him to respond.

"That sounds like a fine idea," Robert said, then grinned.

Jack looked at Miss Ginifer, then smiled.

"It's settled then," Thomas said. "Jack will see you home safely, Miss Ginifer."

"Shall we be on our way then?" Jack held out his arm to Miss Ginifer.

Miss Ginifer's eyes met Thomas', but neither of them said a word. She then turned to Jack and said, "Yes, thank you. I must be getting home."

Robert and Thomas silently watched Jack and Miss Ginifer leave the shop. After they were gone, Robert returned to stocking the shelves. He was very quiet.

"What's wrong, Robert?" Thomas asked, handing him another tin.

"It's nothing," Robert said, and paused before placing the tin on the shelf. "Everything is *exactly* the way it should be," Robert finally said, and smiled.

* * *

∾

CHAPTER 25

TIME FOR A TALL TALE

Some fairy tales are real.

—Harry Finkle

The next day Jack, Lizzy and Robert stayed busy in the shop doing chores and cleaning the floors. Robert had just finished telling them a tall tale about his going 25 years into the future.

Jack and Lizzy laughed, because naturally they didn't believe him. They thought he was simply making up a rather interesting story to entertain them.

Then, to their shock, Robert proved it!

Robert took them directly to the hidden room beneath the library floor. Jack and Lizzy were stunned.

As they climbed down the spiral staircase, Lizzy was in heaven. "Look at all these wonderful books!" she said.

"If you'd cleaned the library properly, this room would have been found years ago," Jack teased.

Lizzy would normally have risen to the bait, but this time she ignored the comment. The books had her full attention.

Robert just laughed. He was glad to be home.

Robert showed them the glowing book, and the magical lever behind it that looked identical to the lever under the shop counter. He explained what it did and advised them to *never* touch it. They all agreed.

Dreamily, Lizzy studied the book titles in the hidden room. She stopped when she came across one particular book. The light blue spine shimmered. Lizzy removed the book from the shelf. It felt extremely cold. When she looked at the front her mouth opened in awe. The cover had been created with sparkles that seemed to dance in the light.

"What's that you've found, Lizzy?" Jack asked. Robert turned to look too.

"It's a special book, I think," Lizzy replied. "The cover has just one word on it: *Snow*." She held the book for them to see. "And it's very cold."

"Blimey!" Robert said.

"You took the words right out of my mouth, Robert," Jack said.

"Do you think it's possible?" Lizzy whispered.

"Do we think what's possible, Lizzy?" Jack asked.

Lizzy paused for a moment, then looked into the hole where the book had been placed. "It is! It really is! Look!"

Jack and Robert peered into the empty space, and they saw it too. Another lever! Just like the one under the shop counter and just like the one behind the book titled *Lightning*.

"Remember the story Father told us about when it snowed? I bet Uncle Harry pulled the lever while Grandfather was telling Father a bedtime story," Lizzy said, smiling.

"Let's try it!" Robert said, reaching for the lever.

"No, you can't!" Jack grabbed Robert's hand and stopped it from moving forward.

"Why not?" Robert and Lizzy asked in unison.

"It's daylight outside. If we want to test the lever, it'll have to be late at night, just like when Father was a boy. Nobody will notice then," Jack said.

"You're right, Jack," Lizzy said. She lowered her eyes and placed the book back on the shelf.

"We will soon though, right, Jack?" Robert urged.

"Yes, of course we will. I'd like to see it snow too," Jack said, ruffling Robert's hair.

"Wouldn't it be grand if Father could see it snow again in summer?" Robert asked.

"Yes, it would. We'll have to plan it one evening and surprise him. That's a great idea, Robert," Jack said.

"I can't wait to one day tell my grandchildren about all the wonderful mysteries we've found," Lizzy said. "Now let's get out of here. We have a lot to do."

Robert lagged behind and made sure Lizzy did not remove the *Book of Memories*. Although the future Lizzy had mentioned wanting to read it, he thought it would be better left alone. He wouldn't mention the *Book of Memories* to Jack or Lizzy unless it was needed.

But Robert wanted to peek inside the mysterious book just one more time. He had a question that had been lingering on his mind. Robert snatched opened the book to reveal its empty pages, then placed a hand on one of them.

"Does Miss Caroline know any of the secrets of Uncle Harry's shop?" Robert whispered. Perhaps it was merely his imagination, but he had to know. She said peculiar things, and even winked at him! More than once, he felt as if she understood the situation and had offered advice.

Letters magically appeared and began to swirl around the page before forming a single word: "Yes."

Robert was taken aback! "What? How is this possible?" Robert hadn't removed his hand. He needed to be quick about things, or Jack and Lizzy would begin to wonder what he was doing.

Out of nowhere lines began to appear. They formed a drawing of Uncle Harry giving Miss Caroline flowers, to imply she was his sweetheart.

The next drawing was of Uncle Harry whispering in her ear for no other person to hear. *Uncle Harry told Miss Caroline about his magical secrets!* Robert thought. *Did he tell her about all of them? Perhaps one day she and I will talk about this. But until then, it looks like Miss Caroline will be helping us keep a watchful eye on the shop.*

Robert decided the *Book of Memories* made it impossible to keep anything secret, but that people are entitled to their secrets. Robert wouldn't tell Jack and Lizzy about the book for now. He'd remember where it was stored, though, in case an emergency required the tremendous power it offered.

As he climbed the steps, Robert decided to grab a few books for Lizzy. Robert placed the books on the desk for Lizzy to read at a later time. Lizzy grabbed Robert into a tight hug and thanked him for showing them a new room full of books.

"I can't breathe, Lizzy," Robert said, gasping for air. Lizzy released her hold on him and laughed.

Jack and Robert rolled the large rug over the floor again, and moved the chairs and table back where they belonged.

"You've had an adventure all by yourself this time, Robert," Jack said. "I'm glad you're back."

"I am too," Robert said, grinning. "But Jack, you were with me the entire time. I wasn't alone.

"There is another thing I want to mention to both of you," Robert added.

"What is it?" Jack and Lizzy asked.

"It's about Mr. Lowsley," Robert said. He told them about Mr. Lowsley burning down Miss Caroline's home, then questioning him in an intimidating way. "Mr. Lowsley is a bad man! He's done many ruthless things! We need to tell someone so he doesn't get away with it!" Robert's face flashed with anger.

"Robert, wait," Lizzy said, then stepped closer and placed a hand on his shoulder to calm him. "Mr. Lowsley hasn't done any of those vile things. Not yet, anyway. You haven't pulled the lever behind the *Lightning* book. So the opportunity for Mr. Lowsley to burn Miss Caroline's home will never come to be."

"You've already changed the future by making sure you don't repeat your mistakes, Robert," Jack said. "Miss Caroline won't lose her home to a fire, Father won't be sick, and Mr. Lowsley will have no reason to enter the shop to offer to buy Miss Caroline's home which means you won't blurt anything out about the hourglasses in front of him. And just to make sure, for future reference, if anything ever happens to the hourglasses and you need help, please, please ask one of us to join you in the storage room."

"I will, Jack," Robert agreed.

"I have no doubt Mr. Lowsley is a low-life who thinks only of himself. I also believe, if the opportunity presented itself, Mr. Lowsley would act in the same manner," Lizzy said with a worried look on her face. "To be on the safe side, we should steer clear of him. He's not to be trusted."

Jack, Lizzy and Robert agreed to maintain a safe distance and keep all conversation with Mr. Lowsley and his mischievous companions at a minimum.

"Do you want to go to the bakery? I'm starving!" Robert said.

Jack laughed. "You're always hungry, Robert. What will we ever do with you?"

* * *

~

CHAPTER 26

SUMMER SNOW

The weather is a curious thing to predict.

—Harry Finkle

R obert woke in the middle of the night and remembered everything that had happened over the past week. All the memories came rushing back so fast it scared him. He wasn't sure if he was 10 years old or 35. Robert sat straight up in bed and looked at his hands and feet. He took note of the size of his fingers and toes, then immediately felt relieved. *Yes, I'm still 10 years old! I'm right where I belong.*

It was still dark outside. He tried to go back to sleep, but he kept tossing and turning. The events kept reoccurring in his mind.

The Jack in the future advised Robert to tell his brother and sister everything if he couldn't change things. But Robert *did* make the changes needed, and everything was good again. He wouldn't make the same mistakes twice.

Robert was grateful that he had the opportunity to fix his bad choices. Not everyone gets a second chance...but this is Finkleton.

Robert got out of bed, put on his slippers and wrapped a blanket around his shoulders. He tiptoed down the hall to Jack's bedroom. As quietly as he could, he turned the handle and pushed the door open.

"Jack, Jack," Robert whispered. "Are you awake?"

Jack wasn't moving. Perhaps he didn't hear Robert enter the room. Robert crept closer to the bed where Jack lay, then placed his hand on Jack's shoulder and lightly shook him.

"Jack, Jack," Robert whispered again. "Are you awake?"

"No, I'm asleep," Jack mumbled.

"You're talking, so you must be awake."

"Go back to bed, Robert," Jack said, and pulled the blanket over his head.

"I can't sleep," Robert said.

"So that means I'm not allowed to sleep?" Jack asked.

Robert didn't reply. He just remained standing next to the bed.

"All right, Robert," Jack said. He sat up in bed and rubbed his eyes. "I'm awake."

"Thanks, Jack."

"I have an idea," Jack said, putting on his dressing gown. "Let's go."

"To where?" Robert asked.

"You'll see."

Robert followed Jack down the hall to Lizzy's room. Jack opened the door, and they made Lizzy wake up too.

"What do you want? It's not even morning yet. Go back to sleep," Lizzy rambled.

"I have an idea," Jack said. "Meet us in the library, and make it quick."

A few minutes later, Lizzy joined Jack and Robert.

"What are we doing in here?" Lizzy asked, pushing the hair away from her face.

"We're going to make it snow!" Jack whispered.

Robert's eyes widened, and Lizzy squealed.

"Keep it down," Jack said.

Jack and Robert moved the furniture and rolled the rug to reveal the hidden door in the floor. Lizzy handed Jack a lit candle.

"I'll be right back," Jack said, then proceeded down the spiral staircase.

Lizzy and Robert stared down into the hidden room, eagerly waiting for Jack to pull the lever behind the *Snow* book. A few moments later, Jack reached the top of the staircase.

"Did you do it? Did you pull the lever?" Robert asked.

"Yes," Jack said.

Lizzy squealed again. "Let's go!"

Jack led the way to their parents' room. The door was slightly ajar. Jack pushed it open and stood in the doorway with Lizzy. Robert walked inside to wake them.

The window drapes were pulled closed, and no fire blazed. In the summer a fire isn't needed. Robert could barely see, though. Jack lifted a candle above his head to help Robert cross the room without tripping over the rug or bumping into anything.

"Father? Father? Are you awake?" Robert whispered, then shook his father lightly. He knew his father wasn't awake because he could hear a low snoring sound escape his mouth.

"Robert, what is it? Have you had a bad dream?" William asked in a sleepy voice, with his eyes still closed.

"No, I haven't," Robert whispered. *I actually did have a bad dream,* Robert thought, *but I won't ever tell you about it.*

"Can't sleep, then, is it?"

"No, that's not it," Robert said. It's true he couldn't sleep and that's why he woke Jack, but it wasn't why he was waking his father.

"What is it then?"

"It's just that..." Robert cleared his throat. "It's snowing outside!"

"That's not possible, Robert. You must be dreaming," William said, still half asleep.

Robert wasn't giving up. "Father, wake up! I said it's snowing outside!" Robert shook his father a bit harder.

"It's true, Father," Lizzy said from across the room, just as Emma opened her eyes.

"What do you mean, it's snowing?" William asked.

"Look!" Robert pulled the drapes back, and Jack and Lizzy entered the room to stand by him next to the window.

"Blimey! It's snowing! It's really snowing!" William said. He jumped out of bed and rushed to the window. "Emma, wake up! It's snowing outside! Look!"

Jack, Lizzy and Robert watched as their father's eyes widened. He laughed and clapped his hands together.

"It's just like when I was a boy!" William said, wiping a stray tear from his eye. "You see, children, I told you Finkleton is a magical place."

Jack, Lizzy and Robert laughed with their father, and enjoyed listening to more of his childhood stories as they watched the snow fall from the sky. The snowflakes melted before touching the ground, but it was still a beautiful sight to see. Far in the distance the glowworms brightened the countryside, which made the snow glisten as it fell from the sky.

After the children filled their eyes and memories with the snow, it was time to finally go to sleep. Lizzy returned to her room. Jack and Robert went downstairs to turn the magical snow lever off.

When they reached the shop, though, Jack said "I'll get the lever, Robert. You can watch the snow until it stops."

So Robert stood in front of the large window enjoying the last minutes of snow. Seeing his father relive his childhood memory made Robert feel wonderful inside. He smiled as he watched the flakes disappear before touching the ground. *It truly is an amazing sight to see,* Robert thought.

Just then Robert noticed two men. They were nicely dressed and appeared to be in their mid-20s. They looked strangely familiar. The taller man nodded his head and smiled as they strolled past the window.

"Great Uncle Harry? Grandfather George?" Robert whispered. Then he hugged himself and smiled.

* * *

∽

CHAPTER 27

LIZZY READS A FAIRY TALE

Let your mind take a holiday once in a while.

—Harry Finkle

The next morning Robert persuaded Jack to go with him to the bakery. Robert could smell the fruit-filled scones in the light morning breeze. It wasn't hard to convince Jack once his nose caught the scent too.

Lizzy didn't mind being left alone in the shop. Actually, she quite enjoyed it. She loved it when nothing could be heard except for the *tick tock* sound from the clock hanging on the wall. She could think better that way.

The shop bell rang, however, breaking Lizzy's solitude. In the doorway a young man stood holding two books. *It's the young man from Mr. Wellington's bookshop!* Lizzy thought excitedly.

"Hello," he said, smiling.

"Hello. Can I help you?" Lizzy asked with a squeaky voice.

"Yes, you can, actually. It took me a few days to find you. I believe I have a couple of things that belong to you." He placed the two books he'd been carrying on the counter. "You left them behind."

Lizzy let out a small squeal—not meaning to, of course. "Thank you! These are my books! I meant to return to Mr. Wellington's shop, but I haven't found the time."

"They are your *friends,* as Mr. Wellington would say." He laughed, and Lizzy giggled. "He's quite a character."

"He's the best," Lizzy said, beaming.

"By the way, have you taken my advice?"

"What advice might that be?" Lizzy asked.

"My suggestion that you read something different, something more fun, perhaps. Like about fairies," he said, grinning.

Lizzy scrunched her nose. *Is he testing me to see if I would actually read something so trivial?* Lizzy wondered. *Or is he serious?* "I'm not sure I have any books about fairies," she said simply.

"I'm sure Mr. Wellington has many books about them. You should browse through them the next time you visit his shop. You might actually enjoy them."

"Perhaps I will, but I'll not make any promises," Lizzy said. Then she smiled.

"Please forgive me, I haven't properly introduced myself. My name is Finian Beanly, but you may call me Fin," he said.

Lizzy's cheeks turned a light shade of pink, "It's very nice to make your acquaintance, Fin, and to finally know your name. My name is Elizabeth Finkle, but I prefer to be called Lizzy."

The shop bell chimed once again. Lizzy and Fin looked to see who had entered. There in the doorway stood the relentless Mr. Lowsley. Lizzy scrunched her nose. She didn't trust Mr. Lowsley and didn't like it when he visited.

Mr. Lowsley strolled casually over to the counter. He smiled at Lizzy, then turned to Fin. "Are you ready, my boy? I must be getting you back to your father."

"Yes, sir, I'm ready," Fin said, and turned to Lizzy. "It was very nice to officially meet you. I hope to see you again soon." Mr. Lowsley had already crossed the room towards the door, impatiently waiting to leave.

"You know Mr. Lowsley?" Lizzy whispered. Her eyes grew wide. She gripped her books as she glanced at the man whose greed threatened to ruin Finkleton.

"Yes, I know him," Fin said, laughing. "He's my uncle."

Lizzy was so taken back that she couldn't say a word. She could barely believe her ears. *Finian Beanly is related to that awful Mr. Lowsley! How could this be possible?* she wondered. *The two of them are completely different!*

Lizzy didn't want to have *anything* to do with *anyone* related to Mr. Lowsley. *But Fin seems like such a nice young man,* she thought. *And it would be nice to talk to someone else about books.*

"I hope to see you again. Maybe I'll run into you at the bookshop?" Fin suggested, then nodded his head to bid Lizzy goodbye.

Lizzy didn't respond. How could she? *Maybe Fin wasn't so bad,* she thought. *Maybe, just maybe, they could be friends. But she still didn't have to like Mr. Lowsley.* Lizzy watched Fin leave the shop, followed closely by his uncle.

Clearing her mind, Lizzy took the books Fin had returned to her and placed them in the library. She noticed the stack of books Robert had brought up from the hidden room. Lizzy slid them aside one by one and read the titles as she went.

The large book on the bottom of the pile caught her attention. Its title was *The Fairies of Finkleton.* This gave Lizzy a bit of a start. *Why would Uncle Harry have a book about fairies?* Lizzy laughed at the ridiculousness of it.

"Fairies aren't real!" she blurted out loud. "They are silly little tales made up for the amusement of children."

Still, the book looks harmless enough, Lizzy thought. *Maybe Fin is right. Perhaps I should try to read something more* fun, *as he put it, and open up my imagination. What could it hurt? Even if I don't enjoy it, I'll at least be able to say that I tried.*

Lizzy picked up the book and held it close to her. She returned to the shop, placed the book on the counter and began flipping through it, not really reading but browsing. Several pages in, she noticed a paragraph in large print:

Fairies are drawn to Finkleton for several reasons: minerals, vegetation and, of course, the weather. They reside in hidden realms beneath the village and rarely show themselves. A person can only enter the realm if invited by a fairy.

"That's too bad, really," Lizzy said out loud. "And I was going to start searching for a fairy realm! Silly me to think I could have found it without a fairy to invite me. What ever came over me?"

Lizzy laughed, then continued to flip through the pages until she came across a page with a small piece of loose parchment in it.

It's Uncle Harry's writing! Lizzy thought with excitement. *Goodness, Uncle Harry tends to scribble notes and leave them in the most peculiar places. This book is turning out to be quite interesting, indeed.* Lizzy read the note:

A word of warning to anyone who reads this: Do not *ever* say a fairy's name out loud. If you do, then be prepared to have that fairy's entire family in your life forever. Some of them are friendly and quite useful, while others are troublesome and quickly become a nuisance. You have been *warned.*

Uncle Harry believed in fairies? How could that be? Lizzy wondered. *He was a sensible man. Why would he believe in such childishness?* Out of the corner of her eye, Lizzy saw a flicker of something. When she quickly turned her head to see what it was, nothing was there. *That's odd. Maybe I need spectacles.*

Lizzy tucked the piece of parchment into the back of the book and returned to browsing it. To her surprise, she found yet more of Uncle Harry's scribbled writing down the side of another page.

Why did he feel the need to write in a perfectly good book? I'd never ruin a book by writing inside it, Lizzy thought. *I* am *curious what Uncle Harry had to say, though.* So Lizzy read the note:

The name of my fairy is Bobletty. He belongs to the Letty family. I call him Bob for short. It annoys him, but he pesters me to no end. He is a lazy little bugger and enjoys peeling the paint off my walls. He clutters up my storage room, then lays around eating. He enjoys causing chaos and leaves crumbs everywhere. His family is quite helpful and tries to keep him under control. But unfortunately Bob is beyond reasoning with and does what he wants. He is worse than a spoiled child.

Lizzy giggled. *Do not ever say a fairy's name out loud! This is simply a tale made up for children. Why would Uncle Harry write such nonsense?* Lizzy wondered.

Lizzy placed her finger on the name Uncle Harry had written in the book. *I'll prove just how ridiculous this is,* she thought. *Then I can tell Fin the next time I see him and have a good laugh about it.*

"Bobletty," she whispered, testing the name out. "Bobletty," Lizzy said more loudly, the name rolling off her tongue.

All of a sudden a flash of light zoomed across the room. A long sparkly trail followed the light in every direction, then disappeared as fast as it had appeared.

The light was fast! It flew around the shop, knocking over some items on one of the displays. Finally the light slowed down and landed on the counter directly in front of Lizzy.

"Fairies in Finkleton," Lizzy whispered. "Father was right! They really *do* exist."

* * *

CHAPTER 28

REMEMBER

Have you ever seen glowworms brighten the
countryside or snowflakes
fall from a warm summer sky?

—Harry Finkle

I n Finkleton it can rain or go dry in the barest
blink of an eye.

Glowworms light the night with a brilliant
green and for some, beloved ghosts can be
seen.

Even in the summer for those held dear, snowflakes will sometimes magically appear.

And fairies come and go without a trace because Finkleton truly is a magical place.

The End

* * *

∾

SNEAK PEAK

Saving Finkleton

(Coming Soon)

∾

CHAPTER 1

STARTING ANEW

Memories live forever.

—Harry Finkle

Sunshine danced through the trees, warming the old woman and her granddaughter sitting on an old log overlooking the valley below. Birds chirped and leaves rustled in the breeze, but no other sound could be heard. The old woman folded her wrinkled hands and rested them on her lap. She closed her eyes and took a deep breath, holding it for just a moment. A low sigh whistled through her lips as she released the air from her lungs.

"Grandmother, what's wrong?" the little girl asked. She twirled a strand of her curly blonde hair between her fingers and waited patiently for her grandmother to respond.

The old woman didn't answer right away. She was tired from the long walk, although she had insisted she was strong enough to travel to the top of the valley. She had wanted to look upon the once-famous English village one last time. After 64 years, she wasn't sure her aging body would be able to make the long journey again.

The old woman opened her eyes and gazed at the valley below, relaxed by the soft warmth of sunshine on her cheeks. "I was enjoying some of my wonderful memories, my dear."

"What sort of memories?"

"Memories of Finkleton," the old woman whispered, almost as if she were speaking to herself.

The little girl scrunched her nose. "Finkleton? Why would anyone want to remember Finkleton?" She frowned at the valley below. "It's dried up and deserted. Why would anyone want to live there, anyway?"

The village of Finkleton no longer existed. The land could no longer grow anything. The stream had stopped flowing, and the farmers and their families had moved away.

Seeing the now-desolate village through her granddaughter's view made the old woman's eyes water. She took another deep breath and blinked several times. Her children and grandchildren never knew the Finkleton she loved. The Finkleton she remembered would never be again.

"I just wish you could have seen Finkleton in its glorious days, my dear," the old woman finally replied. "Finkleton used to be a beautiful and thriving village. The weather was always perfect, and not one family wanted to sell its land and move away. Most folks say 'Mother Nature controls the weather—'"

"Everyone knows Mother Nature controls the weather," the little girl interrupted, then rolled her eyes. "What happened to Finkleton, anyway?"

"It was a long time ago, on a beautiful day." The old woman grinned, then placed an arm around her granddaughter. "I wasn't much older than you are now."

The old woman suddenly stopped and raised a finger for silence. There was a noise behind them in the trees.

"It's probably just a rabbit or something," the little girl said. "Please keep telling me the story."

Just then a young man stepped out into the small clearing directly behind them.

The old woman gasped. She stood and gazed at the young man. She felt a bit more at ease when she saw he was alone, clean, decently dressed... and strangely familiar.

"Hello," the young man said politely. "I'm sorry. I didn't mean to interrupt you."

"Are you lost?" the little girl asked, standing up to be next to her grandmother.

"No," he replied. "I overheard you talking."

"You were eavesdropping!" the little girl accused.

"Emma!" the old woman said, embarrassed by her granddaughter's poor manners.

The young man grinned. "No, I was listening, and you just didn't happen to notice. I wasn't being secretive about it. Huge difference, if you ask me."

"Well, I'm not asking," the little girl huffed, folding her arms and scrunching her nose.

The young man looked towards the valley, then placed his hands in the pockets of his trousers. His smile slowly turned to a frown. His eyes widened with disbelief as he scanned the valley looking for something. His expression showed that he didn't find it.

Silence filled the air once again.

"What happened to it? Finkleton, that is," he finally said, turning to face the old woman. His eyes pleaded for an answer.

"It was destroyed many years ago," the old woman said, accidentally squeaking. She cleared her throat.

"What do you mean, it was destroyed? How and when?" the young man demanded.

"Yes, please continue with the story, grandmother," Emma said. She looked at the young man and raised an eyebrow, daring him to interrupt again.

The old woman and her granddaughter sat back on the log. The young man reluctantly sat at the far end of the log.

"It was about 50 years ago," the old woman said. "It was a beautiful sunny day; the weather in Finkleton was almost always perfect. The light breeze carried the scent of flowers throughout the village. I'll never forget that wonderful smell." She hung her head and sniffed. Emma placed a hand on her grandmother's arm.

"Please, go on," the young man said.

"All at once, the darkest clouds I have ever seen filled the sky," the old woman blurted out. "They came out of nowhere. Thunder roared everywhere, and then lightning began to strike furiously throughout the village. People were screaming and running for shelter!"

The old woman squeezed her hands together before continuing. "Houses caught fire, and thick smoke filled the village. The rain came next. Huge drops poured from the sky. The lightning and rain didn't stop. Water filled the village so fast people barely had time to take their families to higher ground." The old woman gazed at the valley below, lost in thought.

"We watched from this very spot," she continued. "The weather destroyed Finkleton, and there was nothing anyone could do. We lost everything. It was a terrible day, and I've never forgotten. That day changed our lives forever. Nothing has been able to grow in Finkleton since then. Water no longer flows through the village, and the land has dried up."

"How sad," Emma said softly.

"Thank you for sharing your story," the young man said. "It was nice meeting both of you, but I must be getting back." He quickly stood and turned to walk away.

"Where are you going?" Emma asked. "Do you live around here? What's your name?"

The old woman stood and yelled, "Jack! Please wait!"

The young man stopped. He stood still for a moment and took a deep breath. Then he slowly turned to face the old woman, his eyes narrowed with curiosity. "How do you know my name?"

"You can fix this! All of this!" the old woman said with renewed energy, pointing to the valley below. "Find out what happened and make things right. You're here for a reason. You must go back! You must save Finkleton!"

"Who are you?" he whispered.

"Listen to me, Jack!" She pointed an outraged finger at his chest, forcing him to take a step back. "You can bring the magic back to Finkleton!"

"Who are you?" he demanded, cocking an eyebrow.

Emma placed her hands on her hips and interrupted, "Everyone knows my grandmother! Her name is Elizabeth Finkle, but she prefers to be called..."

"Lizzy?" Jack whispered, looking into her eyes.

Lizzy grinned and nodded. She placed a shaky hand on Jack's shoulder. "You can make things right where they once went wrong. Please, Jack," Lizzy pleaded. "It's not too late. You must save Finkleton."

"Tell me everything," Jack said, gesturing for them to sit down. "Start from the beginning."

"It all started with a book," Lizzy said.

"A book?" Jack and Emma asked in unison.

"What sort of book?" Jack asked.

"It was a book about fairies," Lizzy whispered.

* * *

ABOUT THE AUTHOR
K.C. HILTON

Born and raised in Aurora, Illinois I spent my childhood playing street games with the neighborhood kids. When I wasn't outside, I spent much of my time reading and getting lost in adventurous worlds and whirlwind courtships. At the age of seventeen, I moved to Kentucky and eventually began to raise a family of my own.

I have always been entranced by stories of magical adventure. Although I have had to live in the practical world, running a family business as well as two of my own, I have discovered that writing is an entirely new, exciting adventure all on its own!

We have a large family and our get-togethers are so much fun! Did I mention that I'm a photographer? Yes, I take tons of photos! We also have a mini dachshund, her name is "Roxy" and only weighs 10 pounds, but is a huge part of our family. She's so spoiled!

In my spare time, I can be found updating my website or blog, finding great books to read or watching videos. Most days I crave Diet Coke, pizza and chocolate, in no particular order.

Website: http://www.kc-hilton.com

Blog: http://www.themagicoffinkleton.com

CPSIA information can be obtained at www.ICGtesting.com
Printed in the USA
BVOW08s1151271013

334760BV00001B/24/P